SPRING BREAKUP

A So Over the Holidays Novella

ERIN MCLELLAN

Spring Breakup

Print 978-1-7350049-6-9

Ebook ISBN 978-1-7350049-5-2

Editing: Susan Selva

Proofreading: M.A. Hinkle

Cover Artist: Cate Ashwood, http://www.cateashwooddesigns.com

Content Warnings: explicit sex and language; light alcohol consumption; discussion of breakups; natural disaster in the form of an avalanche.

Praise for So Over the Holidays

Bottle Rocket (So Over the Holidays #3)

"Scorching hot! Bottle Rocket *is a story of sexual awakening that fed my femdom fantasies."*

—New York Times bestselling author Skye Warren

"There's a lot to enjoy about this short, steamy, and fun romance … McLellan is always great for sex toy positivity in her books and all her main couples are queer."

—Autostraddle (12 Self-Published LGBTQ Books to Bring to the Beach This Summer

"Erin McLellan does it again with a sexy, Independence Day-themed romp … You'll be cheering for Rosie, Leo, and their summer of love as they get a second chance at happily ever after, fireworks included."

—Layla Reyne, author of the bestselling Fog City Trilogy

"This sexy, fun, LGBTQ sex-positive series continues with another great installment! I loved the banter between the hero and heroine, loved the fast pace, and McLellan's trademark humor and great characterization. This is a solid homerun for me!"

—Annabeth Albert, author of the Hotshots Series

***Candy Hearts* (So Over the Holidays #2)**

"Candy Hearts *by Erin McLellan is sweet, steamy, totally cute and little bit kinky."*

—National Public Radio (For February, 3 Romances That Are Short and Candy-Sweet)

"A super swoon Valentine's Day read with the perfect mix of spice, sweetness, and humor."

—Neve Wilder, author of the Rhythm of Love Series

"Candy Hearts *is blazing hot Valentine's fun that is jam packed with delightful tropes and sex toys. Exactly the level of heat I needed to melt the winter blues."*

—Rachel Reid, author of the Game Changers Series

Stocking Stuffers (So Over the Holidays #1)

"Erin McLellan delivers an authentic portrait of a bisexual woman embarking on a M/F relationship … Stocking Stuffers *belongs in the stocking of any romance reader looking for a fresh take on holiday romance with a healthy side of kink."*

–Entertainment Weekly (19 Christmas Romances to Keep You Warm This Holiday Season)

"The sexual tension sizzled from start to finish. McLellan weaves sex toys, experimentation and curiosity perfectly into the intimate moments between Sasha and Perry … Get this book as a gift to yourself for the holidays!"

–Rachel Kramer Bussel, editor of Best Women's Erotica of the Year Series

"With a Scrooge-like heroine who owns her sexuality with a boldness that is admirable and refreshing, and a sensitive hero who's a lover of romance books and family, Stocking Stuffers is a fun, kinky and yes, swoony, holiday romance packed with laughs, hot sex, emotion and a love that will have you rooting for the happily ever after in ugly Christmas sweaters."

–Naima Simone, USA Today bestselling author

"This book is incredibly steamy yet never loses the Christmas cheer."

—Culturess (5 romance books to read for Christmas in July 2022)

Blurb

After a painful breakup, Tyler needs a vacation. He joins friends on their spring break getaway to Alaska, but the trip doesn't go to plan. Snow, mud, and an avalanche conspire to trap him in a romantic cabin alone with Dean Humphries. Tyler needs time to lick his wounds, and Dean is nothing but an inconvenient temptation.

To protect his heart, Dean masks his feelings behind charm and indifference, but Tyler Vlachos easily sneaks past his defenses. It isn't the avalanche that knocks Dean for a loop. It's the brilliant and heartbroken Tyler.

Stranded together, undeniable chemistry thaws the ice between them. But Tyler, who has trust issues a mile wide, and Dean, who hates letting people in, must break down the barriers around their hearts or leave their love behind in Alaska.

Spring Breakup *is a low-angst, steamy, male/male romance novella with plenty of Alaskan charm, a nerd/artist pairing, forced proximity, and naughty vacation shenanigans.*

To everyone in Alaska who helped me fall in love with the 49th state
—even in the muddy, slushy, miserable spring.

Content Notes

Spring Breakup is a low-angst novella, but there are a few content notes to be aware of: sex and language; light alcohol consumption; discussion of past breakups; and natural disaster in the form of an avalanche (no injuries).

This novella takes place in a fictional Alaskan town.

Chapter One

DEAN HATED THE EVIL-EX STEREOTYPE. It was reductive. He stayed friendly with his exes. Surface-level friendly, you know? He got invites to their weddings and followed their side-hustles on social media.

According to one ex who had psychoanalyzed him during their breakup, "surface level" was a good descriptor of most of his relationships, romantic and otherwise. Dean had been invited to her third child's christening a few weeks ago. He'd sent a personalized jewelry box as a gift.

Of course, he'd heard about bad exes, cheaters and such, but he'd never cared enough to get too bent out of shape when his relationships fell apart, regardless of the reason. Sometimes he was down for a day or so. Sometimes he missed the person when they were gone, but it didn't sucker punch him.

He'd never longed so deeply for someone that he had, say, been inspired to create art about them decades later.

No way. He would leave intensity like that to his best friend, Leo.

And he would leave crying over a man on an airplane to Tyler Vlachos, who was cute as hell, even with red-rimmed eyes and a ridiculous shirt.

Dean didn't know Tyler very well. They'd met once or twice. Surface-level acquaintances, you might say. But Dean was too nosy not to try to get to the bottom of the other man's tears. He hadn't been able to keep his eyes off Tyler for the last leg of their flight to Alaska.

"What's wrong?" he asked Tyler when they'd made it to baggage claim after a very long flight. Rosie and Leo, their travel companions, were too wrapped up in each other to hear.

"What? Nothing," Tyler said.

"Why did you cry for the last two hours, then?"

Tyler gave an exasperated sigh. "I'd planned to visit Alaska with my boyfriend Francis one day, and now I'm doing it without him."

"Oh God, did he die?" Dean asked, horrified. "I'm so sorry."

Tyler shook his head, his messy blond hair sticking to the stubble on his cheeks. "No. We broke up."

"Oh." Unease plucked at Dean's chest. "When?"

Tyler's eyebrows pinched in, and Dean tried not to feel bad about the third degree.

"Last week. He's using this week to move out of my condo. He'll probably nick half my stuff."

Oh, for fuck's sake.

The vacation was a trap.

"Leo!" Dean snapped. Leo jerked his head away from smelling Rosie's hair and sauntered over, looking for all the world like an innocent man. "Why did you invite me on this last-minute spring break trip? Is it a pseudo-charity vacation for lost and broken boys?"

Dean should have been suspicious of the invite. He should have asked questions, but he'd assumed he would get some awesome sex with Rosie and Leo out of the deal, so he hadn't been too fussed.

"What do you mean?" Leo asked, and Tyler's pretty blue eyes ping-ponged between them.

"Did you invite Tyler on this vacation last week as well? After his breakup?"

"We decided to come to Alaska on a whim. We got a deal on the cabin since it's the off-season here," Leo said. Rosie approached and slipped her arm around Leo's waist, giving Dean a don't-mess-with-us glare. Most men would cower, but Dean didn't appreciate getting played. Even by people as hot as Rosie and Leo.

"And you happened to invite two men who each recently went through breakups to the middle-of-nowhere Alaska? On a whim? It was just a coincidence?"

A pinwheel of emotions flew over Tyler's face, and Dean tried very hard not to analyze each one.

"You're going through a breakup too?" Tyler asked. He sounded way too fucking hopeful that they'd get to bond over that bullshit.

"Barely." Dean waved his hand. That wasn't important.

"You were with Viggo for a year," Leo said.

Dean huffed. Viggo was fine. And Dean was more than fine.

"It has nothing to do with your breakups," Rosie said, her voice as cold as the weather outside, so… *frigid.* "You're our friends, and we wanted to spend time with you."

"And no one else said yes," Leo added.

Rosie closed her eyes on a laugh.

Dean had been so excited to spend a week with Rosie and Leo.

And, of course, Tyler, who he was sharing a room with, would be there too.

It was true that Dean had been in a relationship for a year, but it had been one of the loneliest, least inspiring years of his life.

He was in a rut. A relationship rut. A friendship rut. A creative rut where it was a slog to even pick up his pencils. He was in dire need of a reset and the special kind of companionship only Leo and Rosie offered him.

Leo actually knew him, saw him, and it would be a relief to be able to let his guard down.

But he would not be able to let his guard down around Tyler, especially if he thought Dean was some potential love connection.

He turned toward Tyler. It was snowing outside, and the man had on a tropical camp shirt and sandals. Something about that pricked at every annoyance sensor in Dean's brain.

"Whatever our so-called friends planned"—Dean

gestured toward Rosie and Leo—"we are not falling for it."

Tyler blinked. "I don't know what you mean."

Dean clicked his tongue in irritation. "They have a plan. Trust me. I'm not going to be your spring break fling. Your getting-back-up-on-the-horse man of the hour."

Finally, the sadness cleared from Tyler's eyes, and Dean liked the way anger made Tyler's cheeks flush. He liked it way too fucking much.

Damn Rosie. Damn Leo.

"If I want to get back up on the horse," Tyler bit out, "I'll choose a nicer horse."

"I'm nice." Everyone said so. "Did you bring warmer clothes? This is Alaska."

Tyler's mouth dropped open, and he seemed to shake his head in disbelief. Without another word, he grabbed his duffel bag off the baggage carousel and stalked toward the bathroom. Hopefully, to put on long pants and a pair of socks.

Leo threw his arm over Dean's shoulders and said, "That was real smooth, lover."

"Not my best work," Dean admitted. "And I'm still mad at you."

Leo kissed his cheek. "We'll make it up to you later."

Chapter Two

TYLER WASN'T AN IMPULSIVE PERSON. He was thoughtful.

He thought and thought and *thought* about everything from his five-year plan to his grocery list to every trivia question he'd ever missed on national television.

He obsessed over the present and the past. The future… hell, the future took up so much space in his head he was lucky his neck could hold it up.

It wasn't an easy way to live, but in his thirty-two years on this earth, he'd perfected overthinking. It protected him from the unknown. *Usually.*

He wasn't the type of guy to fly off on vacation with only a few days' notice or break up with his boyfriend last week over breakfast without really *thinking* through the repercussions and the fact they lived together and now needed to *not* live together.

Not that Francis had left him much choice.

Tyler's meticulously ordered life was crumbling around him, and he'd gone to Alaska instead of dealing with it. He hardly recognized himself.

He'd expected the cold weather. He'd expected snow. He was enough of a control freak to research the forecast prior to flying across the country. And yes, he'd packed warm clothes. But he hadn't anticipated that Alaska would be so… *greige*. The sky was murky. The roads were covered in muddy slush. The snow was dirty.

It matched his mood. No complaints.

He didn't understand why Rosie and Leo had chosen to go somewhere freezing for spring break, rather than a hot, sandy beach with an open bar. But if it weren't for Rosie, Tyler would currently be staring at the ceiling of his bedroom feeling sorry for himself while his asshole of a boyfriend packed up his belongings and begged for another chance.

Ex-boyfriend.

"There should be mountains there," he said as they drove out of Anchorage and toward their destination, a cabin outside the tiny town of Silverbrite Springs. "The Chugach Mountains."

"Are you sure?" Dean asked. Tyler didn't miss the way Dean seemed to always be watching him. It put Tyler on edge.

"Yes," he said. Of course, he was sure. They were covered in low-hanging clouds, but they were there.

Tyler was a quintessential know-it-all. He felt the snarky monster inside him gearing up for a fight. That snarkiness had been trampled down lately, but it was still there. The problem was that Dean tongue-tied him, even before insinuating the trip was some grand matchmaking plan by Rosie and Leo.

A plan Dean was obviously opposed to. He'd made his disinterest super clear.

Dean was gorgeous, clever, and confident. He had an almost-invisible cleft lip scar at his cupid's bow, slightly shaggy brown hair, a sexy voice, and dark eyes. His smile was always rakish and did funky things to Tyler's stomach. The first time they'd met—at a county fair where Rosie had submitted a peach jam for judging—Tyler had been struck by Dean's carefree laugh. The next day, during their lunch break, Rosie had mentioned that Dean was in Leo's newest art book as a model, and Tyler hadn't been able to resist buying the book for himself.

Francis had been shocked and hadn't let Tyler keep the book of erotic art on the coffee table, even though it was a coffee table book. Now Tyler could keep whatever the hell he wanted on the coffee table. Except the table was Francis's, so Tyler would need to buy a new one.

Fuck, he would open that book up to Dean's page—a watercolor painting of Dean's strong hand wrapped around a dick—and leave it on the floor of his living room for all to see.

Strangely buoyed by that thought, Tyler relaxed. He wasn't going to let Dean or Francis ruin the gift of a week away from the outside world. He'd have six days where he wouldn't have to look at a lesson plan. Six days without answering to school administrators or cleaning up after an untidy child. Six days without Francis nagging him about his clothes or his taste in TV. Six days of nature and wine and hanging out with Rosie. That was cause enough to celebrate.

For the whole drive to Silverbrite Springs, Tyler daydreamed about their cabin, the soapstone fireplace, the barrel sauna, and sharing a room with Dean. Everything would go flawlessly. Nothing would be awkward. Tyler would have fun and be chill and cool. It would be great.

Then they arrived. Tyler stepped out of their rented van and slipped ass over teakettle into the mud.

Not chill. Not cool. Not great.

Leo hurried over to help him back onto his feet. Tyler's butt and the back of his coat were wet and covered in gray mud. Dean moseyed over and reached the group as Tyler finished a long litany of curses.

Tyler's hair was all over his face, and he went to swipe it out of his eyes.

Dean caught Tyler's wrist. A stunned silence followed. Dean's hand—*that hand, yes*—was bigger than any hand had a right to be.

"Mud." Dean flipped Tyler's palm up to show that it was covered.

Tyler's breath hitched, and he nodded. Dean let him go and stepped back. Tyler glanced up, a thank-you on the tip of his tongue, but Dean took a bigger step back like he couldn't get away fast enough.

Ouch.

Cool, chill, great.

Tyler's hair was still in his eyes, and he tried to blow it away. Rosie rushed to assist, brushing it aside.

A door opened at the cabin to their right, and Tyler turned gratefully toward the stranger who emerged. He was embarrassed and latched on to the distraction like a lifeline.

There were four cabins along the driveway lane, three for guests and one for the owner of the resort. The guest cabins were private and obscured by the trees, barely visible except for their hot-pink doors. The host's cabin was simpler and easily seen from the gravel road. Tyler clocked the rainbow flag in the front window, his brain zeroing in on the small comfort.

A young woman wearing a T-shirt and seemingly unaffected by the cold came down the steps from the host's cabin and waved at them. "Oh, bad luck. That glacial silt is slippery. Are you okay?" She reached them and shook their hands, except Tyler's, because his were filthy. "That silt will brush off your clothes once it's dry, but I also have a washer and dryer you can use if that doesn't work."

"Thanks," Tyler mumbled.

"I'm Brooks Rossi, by the way," the woman continued. "Part-owner of Chum Smoke Cabins. I'm around most days if you need anything. I've lived in Silverbrite Springs my whole life, so I'm a good source of info. But there's also a welcome packet in the cabin full of information about the town, our property, and seasonal activities." She shot them a bright, crooked smile.

Brooks had an appealing outdoorsy vibe. Tyler had a feeling she probably knew how to pitch a tent in the rain and clean a fish. She oozed confidence and competence.

"You might see my brothers, Wrangell and Sarg, around," Brooks continued. "They're my handymen. But you're the only guests, so you'll have a lot of privacy. We won't come bothering you unless you need bothering."

They exchanged more chitchat before Brooks left them to settle in. As soon as they were out of earshot, Dean said, "So she's gorgeous."

Tyler was too tired to spend another second gossiping. It had been a long day of plane rides and car rides and falls in the mud. He was ready to sleep. He made his way to the cabin to wash off.

A few minutes later, Rosie peeked through the doorway of the bathroom where he was washing his hands. "You okay?"

Tyler tried to smile at her. Rosie was his best friend. Though he would never tell her that. The news would shock her. They rarely hung out outside of the breakroom at the elementary school where they worked.

But his happiest moments in the last year were the fifteen minutes before school when they chatted over cups of decaf in the teacher's lounge. Which was saying something *loud* about all his other relationships.

"I'm fine."

She gave him a gentle smile full of pity he pretended not to see. It was bad enough to fall in a mud puddle in general, but doing it in front of Rosie's hot partner, Leo, and hot friend, Dean, was absurd.

He dried his hands and gingerly removed his coat so the mud on the back of it didn't get on anything in the bathroom.

Rosie took the coat from him, and they examined it. The mud—glacial silt—had in fact dried already, and it flaked off easily. They quickly brushed it off over the shower drain and used the showerhead to wash it away. He needed to change pants but had left his bag in the van in his rush to get his hands clean.

"Have you talked to Francis?" Rosie asked.

Tyler wrinkled his nose and touched a tiny toucan near the bottom of his shirt. "Oh, he's texting me a play-by-play of moving out. He's pretty disappointed I took a vacation rather than sticking around to work through our problems. I told him I have bad service out here but haven't checked my phone to see if it's true."

Dean appeared over Rosie's shoulder and said, "It's true. I've only got one bar off and on." He held up Tyler's duffel. "Bag."

Tyler willed himself not to remember the way Dean's hand had felt around his wrist outside. But, of course, his brain didn't cooperate, pulling up the sense memories like a 5D movie. The scrape of rough calluses on his pulse point. The scent of ice and mud and Dean's deodorant working hard after a long, long travel day. The melodic voice that seemed at odds with Dean's frown.

Too much *thinking*.

“Thanks.” Tyler took his bag and dug through it for a pair of sweatpants.

Dean leaned against the doorjamb of the bathroom, and Rosie stood there holding his coat. Neither got the hint that he wanted to get his muddy clothes off… privately.

“Are you sure you and this Francis guy are completely over?” Dean said. “Maybe you should have brought him. Tried to reconnect out in the romantic Alaskan wilderness.”

“And if I’d brought a plus-one, where would you sleep? We’re sharing a room.”

Dean winked at Rosie and said, “In my experience, king beds can sleep three.”

Tyler was scandalized by that. Was Dean saying he would share with Tyler and Francis in this scenario? Because that would not have happened. They weren’t nearly exciting enough for that.

Rosie smiled and shook her head as if she was charmed by Dean’s antics. Tyler loved Rosie’s sense of humor, but he was usually let in on the joke. He wasn’t in on *this* joke.

Screw this. He yanked his pants down so he was in nothing but boxers.

Neither Dean nor Rosie seemed fazed by him undressing in front of them. He pulled up his sweatpants and started to unbutton his shirt. It was cold in the cabin, and while it pained him to lose the comfort of his typical wardrobe, he needed long sleeves.

Dean watched him absently, his gaze moving over

Tyler's chest. It felt… almost careless, like Tyler wasn't even there. Like his body was just a body and not connected to a human being. Dean's expression was totally blank.

"Like what you see?" Tyler asked, fed up enough to be rude.

Dean didn't say a word, but he left.

Chapter Three

DEAN'S PALMS PRICKLED. He could feel the shape of compressed charcoal between his fingers. He imagined the scratch of the tip along expensive paper as he sketched the silly birds on Tyler's shirt.

Tyler had snarked at him in the bathroom, and Dean had gotten that hot feeling in his throat that was either annoyance or interest. He wanted it to be annoyance, so he was very *annoyed* with himself that it didn't seem to be.

"Do you have your artsy stuff with you?" Rosie asked, meaning his pencils and drawing pad. Dean wasn't like Leo. He wasn't good enough to sell his art, and he hadn't been inspired to draw outside the classes he taught in ages. But he always brought supplies when he traveled, just in case.

"I do."

"That's lucky."

"Why?" he grumbled.

"No reason," she sang.

She left him standing in the middle of the room and curled up in Leo's lap on a leather couch. Dean took the opportunity to look around. He'd already checked out the room he'd be sharing with Tyler—nice-quality linens, fluffy pillows, cedar ceiling, a small loveseat, and a large window. The cabin was two stories with a big, open living space that included a simple kitchen, a kitchen table, and two sofas framing a cast-iron stove as their heat source, which Leo had gotten up and running. According to Brooks, the stove had a soapstone that only required one or two big fires a day to keep the cabin toasty.

"How's your room?" Dean asked.

"Nice. Lots of windows and a balcony with a great view of the lake. There's an outdoor heater out there too," Leo said. He was nuzzling into Rosie's neck, and Dean longed to plop down there and get some attention.

"So… with Tyler here, are we going to—I mean… does he know that we sometimes…" Dean shook his head.

"I love it when you blush, Dean. Does Tyler know we fuck sometimes?" Rosie asked as matter-of-fact as ever.

"Yeah. That." He wasn't sure where everything stood. Rosie and Leo were one of the only constants in his life. His only deepish relationship. He couldn't imagine a week in close proximity to them without being… in close proximity to them. It had been a year, and he'd missed them.

Rosie lifted a delicate shoulder. "We're not going to be doing it in the kitchen while we make dinner. We'll control ourselves until it's appropriate."

"Speak for yourself," Leo teased and kissed her neck.

Rosie and Leo were in love with each other. *Only* each other.

Dean would be lying if he said he hadn't, at certain moments, wished they were interested in more than simply fucking him. It was so comfortable when he was in their bed. So easy.

Too easy maybe. There was no romantic spark between the three of them. That spark existed between Leo and Rosie alone. Dean was just lucky enough to experience its warmth every once in a while.

"I want you to blow me on that balcony, Dean," Leo said. "No one gives head like you."

That was exactly what Dean wanted. To be close to his friends. To make them feel good. To enjoy something uncomplicated that put no expectations on him.

He never lived up to expectations.

"You flatterer."

The bathroom door opened, and they all turned toward Tyler. A frown pulled at Dean's lips. Tyler looked cozy in aqua sweatpants and an oversized black hoodie. His hair was staticky and wild. Dean couldn't help but notice the way Tyler's body filled out those ridiculously bright sweatpants.

"Uh. Hi." Tyler said. He lifted up his duffel bag. It was full of books. Trivia books. Dean had seen them when he'd gotten it out of the van. "Which room am I in?"

"I'll show you." Dean shooed him toward their room, and they went in together.

Tyler's eyebrows dropped and lifted in quick succession. "That's a queen bed."

"So?"

"You said it was a king. You said three could fit in a king, so I expected a king."

"Oh, sorry." Rosie and Leo were the ones with a king mattress. He'd been talking about—*joking* about—sleeping with them. "You could sleep on the loveseat if not having those extra five inches of mattress space is such a problem."

"It's sixteen inches."

"What?"

Tyler tilted his chin up. "The difference between a queen and king is sixteen inches in width."

Did Tyler sell mattresses? Why the hell would he know that?

Dean thought he was a special education teacher.

"And you need those sixteen inches in order to sleep with… next to me?"

"Extra inches aren't necessary. Most people don't know how to use them correctly anyway."

Dean willed himself not to jump headfirst into flirtatious banter. He wasn't falling for it. He needed *friendship*. He needed Rosie and Leo. He did not need to lead on sweet, sappy, heartbroken Tyler Vlachos.

"*You* could sleep on the loveseat," Tyler said before Dean was able to make his mouth work again.

"Do either of us have to sleep on the fucking loveseat?"

"It's not actually a loveseat. It's a chaise lounge."

Dean almost asked what the difference was because he was certain Tyler had some bizarre answer. But Dean couldn't handle Tyler being all smart and cute and weird, so he left the room instead.

He was pretty excellent at walking away. He'd had a lifetime of examples to learn from.

Chapter Four

TYLER WOKE UP WITH A START, his heart pounding. He was alone. Dean Humphries was nowhere to be found. He wasn't in bed or on the chaise.

Tyler checked the time on his phone. It was midnight. He'd gone to bed early, the long travel day plus an emotional week catching up with him before everyone else was ready to call it a night.

He didn't like not knowing where Dean was. His brain shot through a million terrible scenarios. None of them were good. They varied from low stakes—Dean, Rosie, and Leo had stayed up to talk about Tyler behind his back—to high stakes—an ax murderer had pulled Dean through the window and chopped him up.

He hadn't been looking forward to sharing a bed with Dean.

Okay, there was a small, secret thrill to the idea that they might migrate toward each other in their sleep. Tyler imagined being aggravated by Dean cuddling with him. He imagined Dean's huff when their skin brushed. He imagined them both secretly liking it but pretending it was awful when they woke up entwined.

Shit, Tyler needed to jerk off or something.

He got dressed and peeked into the living room. It was empty. He moved around the downstairs, doing a quick survey.

Dean wasn't in their room, the bathroom, kitchen, or living room. Tyler assumed Rosie and Leo were upstairs together. He heard quiet conversation through the ceiling, but there was no reason for Dean to go into their bedroom.

Maybe Dean was in the sauna or hot tub.

Tyler just had to *know*.

He pulled his coat on, shoved his feet into his boots, and slipped outside. Dean wasn't in the hot tub. It had the cover on.

Tyler walked down the stairs of the porch and glanced up at the cabin's second floor. There was a dim light on in the upstairs bedroom, but Tyler couldn't see anyone through the paneled glass door that led out onto the balcony.

He decided to check the barrel sauna to be sure. Once he was sure, he'd be able to go back to sleep without worrying that Dean had sleepwalked into the woods and been stomped by a moose.

Tyler left their cabin's private alcove to reach the sauna. He knocked. No answer. It was pitch black and empty on the inside.

"Everything okay?" a deep voice asked. Tyler yelped and about jumped out of his skin.

He spun around and saw Brooks and a huge, lumberjack of a man coming down the steps of her cabin.

"Hi. Yes. It's fine."

"Tyler, right?" Brooks said.

"Yes."

"This is my brother Wrangell. We're walking over to the lake to see if we can see the lights. Want to join us?" she asked. Brooks was wearing a long-sleeved T-shirt, and Tyler wondered how she wasn't freezing her butt off. It had to be below freezing. Wrangell at least had on a thick flannel shirt and beanie.

"What lights?"

"The aurora is out. At least according to the Silverbrite Springs group chat." Wrangell held up his phone.

"You have a group chat with the whole town?"

Brooks and Wrangell both laughed at that, but Tyler wasn't sure what was so funny.

"Come with us," Wrangell said. "Most people go their whole lives without seeing it."

Tyler could barely make their cabin out through the trees. "Let me tell my friends where I'm going."

He called Rosie, but there was no answer. She probably had her phone on silent. He sent a text explaining where he was and that they could see the northern lights if they walked to the lake. He also asked if Dean was with them.

Part of him wanted to keep searching for the man,

but he wasn't Dean's babysitter. They weren't even friends.

Tyler followed Brooks and Wrangell across the street and down to the bank of the lake. They stood in silence with their heads turned toward the sky. Eventually, Wrangell lifted a hand and pointed.

"Clouds?" Tyler whispered. He didn't need to whisper, but it felt appropriate to be as hushed as possible.

"No. Wait for your eyes to adjust. It's green," Brooks said. She was also whispering.

Tyler studied the brother and sister. It was dark, but he could see the family resemblance. They were both tall and strong and seemed content in their own skin. He wondered if the other brother resembled Wrangell with his barrel chest and huge arms because that was an intimidating thought. Wrangell looked like he could win a strongman competition.

"There." Wrangell pointed again. "It's moving."

Just as Tyler was starting to feel discouraged, a wisp of pink slithered through his field of vision. Both Wrangell and Brooks gasped. The wisp moved like it was in the current of a river, rippling, and suddenly, Tyler could see it all. The colors unraveled across the dark sky directly over the mountains across the lake. Greens and the occasional pink dancing together, ribbons of movement coming and going, dim and then swiftly bright again.

Tyler realized he'd been holding his breath. He plopped down on a wooden stump that had been placed around the firepit for seating.

"I should go get my friends," Tyler said, but he

couldn't make himself stand. He didn't want to miss anything. He didn't want to blink, much less leave.

Neither Brooks nor Wrangell responded. They were standing shoulder to shoulder, leaning into each other, in their own world.

As swiftly as Tyler had been able to see the aurora, it disappeared.

No one said anything for several long minutes. Tyler kept hoping it would come back. Maybe he should have tried to take a picture, but he had no idea if his phone would have picked it up. He already felt as if the experience was slipping away from him.

Wrangell sighed. "We better go find our wayward brother." His voice, though it was directed at Brooks, made Tyler jump.

"Yeah," Brooks said. "Rock, paper, scissors?"

They played a quick game. Wrangell groused when he lost, but he raised a hand to Tyler. "It was nice to meet you."

"You too. And thank you for this. I would have missed it without you."

Wrangell gave a sort of friendly grunt, then left Tyler and Brooks to cross the street and climb into an old truck.

"Will it come back?" Tyler asked.

"What?" Brooks said

"The lights."

"Oh. Yeah, maybe." She was gazing across the lake, but Tyler suspected she wasn't seeing it. "It's a good forecast tonight. The best night for a few days. It's supposed to rain tomorrow."

"Rain? Not snow?"

"Yep. Rain. We call it spring breakup. The snow's melting, temperatures are rising, and river ice is breaking up. Everyone is antsy for warmth and the midnight sun, but it's still cold enough for hard freezes every other day. It's the worst time of year. Winters are long, and spring is slow," Brooks said. She stomped on a tuft of snow. "You see that red beacon flashing in the middle of Skipper Lake? That's our groundhog, telling us we have several more weeks of miserable, muddy, slushy spring."

"I don't understand."

"Once the ice melts, that beacon falls into the lake. Then it's summer, and we celebrate. I can't wait. I need some vitamin D that doesn't come from a medicine bottle." Brooks turned to him with a smile. "At least the view doesn't suck."

"No. It doesn't suck at all. It's beautiful here."

"I tend to take it for granted, but it's nice seeing it through our visitors' eyes. I'm gonna head back inside. You're welcome to stay out here. Hopefully, the lights will come back before the rain moves in."

Tyler let his eyes drift back over the lake and the mountains and up to the sky. "Yeah. Thank you."

"Sure thing." Brooks left him in peace, and it really did feel like peace.

TYLER WAITED for the aurora borealis to reappear for

thirty minutes before it got too chilly to endure. He let the moonlight lead him back to the cabin.

Seeing the aurora was enough to convince him to take advantage of his spring break. He needed to shed the sadness and embarrassment about his breakup, forget Francis, and move on.

As he passed the sauna, their cabin towering in front of him, he heard a noise. A choking sound.

His pulse sped up as he looked for the source.

It happened again, but this time with a light laugh.

Tyler's body reacted before his mind. His face went hot. His heart jumped into his throat. He immediately stepped into the shadows of the spruce trees and out of the moonlight.

He spotted the culprits. Leo, Rosie, and Dean were on the second-story balcony. There was a lamp on in the bedroom, backlighting them. They had three steaming mugs lined up on the balcony railing, and they were all bundled up with blankets and hats. They didn't have the outdoor heater on, but the chill in the air certainly hadn't deterred their extracurriculars.

Dean was on his knees for Leo and had been the source of the choking sound.

Rosie was observing from a chair, and Tyler heard her voice, light and amused, but he couldn't make out the words.

Tyler started shaking. It was from the chill.

Probably. Maybe.

Even though he didn't feel cold at all anymore.

Leo let out a muffled sort of shout, and seconds later, Dean sat back on his heels.

Oh God. Tyler needed to stop watching.

It was no skin off his nose if Rosie liked to watch her partner get sucked off by other dudes. To each their own. It was pretty hot from where he was standing and surely hotter up close.

Tyler took a deep breath and made his way out of his hidey-hole in the trees. But as Tyler stepped back onto the path, Dean knee-walked toward Rosie and dove under the blanket that was thrown over her lap.

She tipped her head back, and the lamplight from their room gilded her neck in gold.

Tyler scurried behind another tree and closed his eyes. The bark was rough against his back. His cock was so hard it hurt.

Tyler felt… confused. Rosie was his best friend, and yeah, they didn't talk about their sex lives, but the fact that she was getting eaten out by Dean Humphries on a balcony was a bit of a surprise. But what confused him the most was how turned on he was.

Tyler was a dyed-in-the-wool gay guy, but proficiency was sexy. And if Rosie's soft, happy sounds were any indication, Dean was proficient as fuck.

Was that what this vacation was for them? A chance to fool around?

Was it going to be a big secret they kept from him for the whole freaking week?

He hated that thought.

It was too much. Too much to process. And frankly,

now he didn't care because he could hear Rosie's increasingly desperate noises.

Tyler unbuttoned his pants and pulled himself out. It didn't take but a handful of strokes to get to the edge. He bit his wrist as he crashed into his orgasm.

It felt good but wasn't satisfying.

Story of his sex life.

He got himself back under control quickly. He prided himself on that.

It sounded less frantic on the balcony, just hushed voices having a conversation.

He couldn't hang out in the forest all night. He chanced another glance at the cabin. They were standing, but Dean had his back against the railing. Leo was looking out toward the lake, and Rosie was facing Dean, pressed close to him. *Cozy*. At least the funny business was over.

Tyler crept out of the trees and made for the center of the driveway. He didn't want to sneak up on them.

Leo spotted him first and gave him a lazy wave. "Hey, man. Where you been?"

"I was watching the aurora borealis with Brooks and her brother. I texted and called Rosie," Tyler said.

Dean seemed to stiffen, but that might have been Tyler's imagination. He didn't turn around or acknowledge Tyler, which jabbed at Tyler's insecurities.

Rosie whispered something in Dean's ear before smiling down at Tyler. "I haven't checked my phone in a few hours. I'm sorry. I would have loved to have seen that!"

Tyler doubted that. She had been having her own fun. Though he would take the northern lights over most orgasms any day. He nodded and smiled up at her.

"I like you in glasses," Leo said, and Tyler's whole body flushed at the compliment. He hadn't put his contacts in when he'd started his fruitless Dean search. Obviously, Dean had been with Leo and Rosie the whole time. "Why don't you come up and have a nightcap with us?"

Was that a euphemism? Surely not. They seemed… well… *done*.

Dean still hadn't turned around. It felt deliberate, but Tyler didn't have the energy to analyze everything. Not tonight. Not after his own hurried orgasm was making him slow and groggy.

"That's okay. I'm tired. Maybe tomorrow night."

Leo and Rosie said their goodnights.

Dean did not.

Tyler made his way inside the cabin, ignored the stairs to the second story, and went to bed.

Chapter Five

"YOU'RE SO MEAN, DEAN," Rosie said in his ear. "You didn't even tell Tyler sweet dreams."

Leo laughed. "You're the mean one, Rosie. Holy shit."

Dean squeezed his eyes shut as Rosie took over and moved the Fleshstroker down his cock. He'd heard the door shut behind Tyler as he'd reentered the house. When Tyler had appeared below them after having evidently been out and about at the lake in the middle of the night, Rosie had leaned in and told Dean to "*Keep going.*"

Dean didn't always enjoy being bossed around in bed, but being controlled by Rosie was a treat he indulged in occasionally. Slipping the masturbation sleeve over himself minutely while Rosie and Leo had talked to Tyler had been its own special and horrible torture.

"Could he tell?" Dean asked.

"That you were jerking off?" Rosie asked.

"Yeah." He didn't know what he wanted the answer to be. He was keyed up. He had Leo's and Rosie's tastes on his lips and Tyler's clipped, smarty-pants voice in his ears.

"I doubt it," Rosie said. "He didn't seem scandalized."

Leo pressed into Dean's other side and licked his earlobe. Dean had missed nights like this with Leo and Rosie. Nights where they fucked and drank and painted. "Too bad," Leo whispered. "Tyler needs a little scandalizing."

"God, please stop talking about Tyler," Dean gritted out.

"Why?" Rosie asked, and Dean knew he was in trouble. She saw him way too clearly for comfort.

"It's going to put me off this awesome orgasm you're building up."

Rosie made a noise in the back of her throat. "Bullshit."

"If I were going to paint Tyler, I'd put him in those glasses," Leo said. Dean bit back a groan. "You didn't get to see him, Dean. Shame really. He's very cute in them."

"Oh, that's a good idea," Rosie said as if she wasn't absolutely tormenting Dean. She moved the Fleshstroker faster over his cock. "What else would you paint?"

Dean shook his head, but it was fruitless. They were ignoring him.

"Well, he would be shirtless. I bet he's got blond chest hair. Beautiful." Leo continued on, but Dean felt like he was underwater. Sound was muffled and distorted.

He didn't want to hear about how Leo would paint Tyler. If Dean were going to draw Tyler, he'd draw him relaxed because it was so different from the man he'd seen so far. He would draw Tyler tumbled back on white pillows, tropical camp shirt open, hair sweaty, eyes closed.

No, eyes *open* but hooded and tired. Satisfied. His lips would be parted and wet, his legs splayed, and—

"That's it," Rosie said in Dean's ear as he started to come, his orgasm endless and slow as syrup. "You're okay."

Leo's arms came around him as Dean's legs wobbled, and Dean gratefully hid his face in Leo's shoulder.

Rosie rubbed his back as the last shudders washed through him. It was all very gentle, which wasn't their usual MO.

He wasn't sure he liked it.

Once Dean had caught his breath, Leo and Rosie led him back inside. They were taking lots of care with him, and he needed them to stop.

"I'm fine," Dean said. "That was hot." Just empty words. Something he often said once the dust had settled on sexual shenanigans. That simple handjob on the balcony had left him feeling fragile, not hot.

"Yeah. Here, lie down," Leo said. "Let us baby you for a change."

Dean was already halfway down, but Leo's words made him spring back up.

Rosie shot him a hard look. "I want to cuddle, so lie down."

Dean followed orders. It was easier when it wasn't for his benefit.

They chatted about nothing for a while, twined together in a friendly puddle on Rosie and Leo's bed, and it felt so nice and normal. Dean ate it up, soaked in the goodness and friendship.

Leo fell asleep first, his snores familiar.

"How do you sleep next to that ruckus?" Dean said teasingly.

"He travels a lot. Makes it easier."

They both laughed, and Rosie rolled to directly face Dean.

"So… about Tyler," she said cautiously.

Dean did everything in his power not to stiffen. "What about him?"

"He's a great guy. He's going through a rough breakup."

"I'm aware. I'm also going through a breakup. We've discussed this."

Rosie rolled her eyes. "But you're *you*. You're always fine."

Dean nodded, even as a hidden part of his heart rebelled. He was fine, but… *No*, he was fine. And it was good that people recognized that.

"And Tyler isn't?" Dean asked.

"He will be. He's better off, but it hurts to be hurt. You should be nice."

"I'm nice."

"You're the nicest guy I know. Which is why it's weird

that you're so"—Rosie fluttered her hand—"*whatever* it is you are about him."

"That makes no sense."

"Sorry. Three orgasms does that to me."

Leo had given her the first two before they'd moved out onto the balcony. Dean had been fortunate enough to give her a third.

"Lucky girl."

Rosie chuckled sleepily. "You're a nice guy… Tyler's a nice guy. So, you know… be nice together."

That sounded like a warning, so Dean took it as one. "Gotcha."

"Staying?" she asked as her eyes closed. He never stayed the night with them and didn't plan on it now.

Except *Tyler* was in his bed, which was a recipe for disaster.

"We'll see," Dean said, but she was already asleep.

Dean did try to sleep in the big king bed with Rosie and Leo, but his mind kept wandering. Surely, Tyler had noticed that Dean hadn't come downstairs.

Not that it mattered what Tyler thought. It didn't matter at all.

Tyler probably slept in pajamas with parrots on them. And he probably snored louder than Leo. And he was probably a blanket hog to boot.

Dean slipped out of Leo and Rosie's bed, tiptoed downstairs, threw a log into the stove, and climbed into bed with Tyler.

Tyler didn't stir.

Dean expected to toss and turn all night, but he was

quickly lulled to sleep by Tyler's steady breaths and warm body.

THE NEXT MORNING, they finished their breakfasts, bundled up, and walked out into the slushy snow. Tyler looked around with fresh eyes after his late-night excursion. He'd woken up late and alone, the other side of the bed cold and unrumpled. Dean had obviously never come to bed. He didn't know how to process the information he'd learned last night, and it was hard to pretend he wasn't in on the secret. The whole world felt different and new in the daylight.

The lake was still iced over. He spotted the firepit and rustic benches where he'd sat last night. Mountains covered with heavy blankets of snow surrounded their little slice of heaven from all sides, but they couldn't see the peaks, as they were shrouded in dark, ominous clouds. It was warmer than yesterday. The taste of rain was in the air.

At the crossroads of the driveway and the gravel road, there was a large wooden sign that pointed the opposite direction from which they'd driven in. It said that the town of Silverbrite Springs was only three-quarters of a mile.

The plan was to follow the road into town and enjoy the break in the rain that had moved through in the middle of the night. While they were in Silverbrite Springs, they planned to grab lunch from the one place that sold lunch in the off-season and get a drink from the one place that served drinks.

After a few minutes of walking in silence, Dean said, "Can you imagine living somewhere with such a long winter?"

"It's spring. Spring always starts on March nineteenth, twentieth, or twenty-first," Tyler said, then internally cringed. He couldn't help himself. Francis had hated when he'd spouted random facts.

"There's snow on the ground. That's winter," Dean said.

"Not technically." What was it that Brooks had said last night? *Winter is long, and spring is slow.*

Dean stared at him for a long second, but Tyler couldn't read his expression.

"Seasons are really just *feelings*, don't you think?" Leo said, voice full of levity. "My heart is telling me it's winter." Leo slung his arm around Dean's waist, and they walked ahead.

Tyler couldn't help but read into every touch between the men, every glance between Dean and Rosie. He was nervous to broach the topic with Rosie but felt like he should.

Hey, so how was the sex last night? It looked fun from my angle.

"Bears wake up and leave their dens occasionally when water from snowmelt is dripping into their dens," Tyler rattled off like he was reading from a book. Then he gestured toward a spruce tree that was dribbling water from the tip of a branch. The *plop, plop, plop* of melting snow was everywhere once you started paying attention.

"We'll talk loud so the wet, lethargic bears hear us coming." Rosie smiled.

Tyler scrubbed his face. He felt rough.

She gave his hand a quick squeeze. "Every morning, my kindergarteners arrive at the door with bows in their hair and tucked-in shirts. Their shoes are tied. Their clothes are clean. They're ready to face the day. Fresh as daisies."

"Kindergarteners are the cutest."

She hummed. "By the end of the day, their hair is a disaster, their clothes are a mess, and they have dirt on their faces. They've lost shoelaces and barrettes and jackets. It's one of my favorite things, seeing that change by three p.m."

"Why?"

"Because it means they've learned hard *and* played hard."

Tyler was not following the point of this anecdote. "Give it to me straight here, Rosie."

She laughed. "You look like my kindergarteners. But I think you've only learned hard. Maybe it's time to play hard too."

"In what way?"

Rosie pulled him to a stop. Dean and Leo were horsing around on a higgledy-piggledy row of boulders lining the road. There was a light sprinkle from the rain clouds above, but it wasn't unpleasant. It felt like walking through the vegetable aisle at the grocery store when they turned on the misters.

"What do you enjoy doing outside of work?"

Tyler picked up a smooth rock and skipped it across the thin ice of the lake. "God, I have no idea."

Honestly, who had time for hobbies in this economy? Tyler got home and worked on IEP paperwork, wrote up lesson plans, and tried to save his failing relationship. His job took up the brunt of his emotional bandwidth. His thief of an ex had taken up the rest.

"We should go to trivia night," Rosie said, grabbing his hand again and dragging him back into a walk. Rosie was much more physically demonstrative outside of work, and he was soaking it up.

"I have a team already, but they'll probably kick me off." God, Tyler hadn't even thought of that. His trivia team consisted of Francis's friends from college, plus him.

"They'd kick the *Jeopardy* champion off the team?" Rosie said.

"Well, I'm sure they expect me to bow out gracefully for Francis. They don't care about winning, so my trivia stardom is inconsequential."

"I'll be on your trivia team. We can recruit Benji and William. They'd be good at questions about… I don't know… reality TV and cars?"

"Your hot brother and his hot boyfriend will be too distracting for me to answer any questions myself."

"Gross."

Tyler laughed. He would love to be on a team with Rosie and anyone she deemed worthy.

"Also, I can cover the pop culture questions," he said. "What we need is someone good at mythology. I suck at that." He'd missed a final *Jeopardy* question about mythology once.

"I'll put out feelers. I bet we can find the perfect person. Maybe Dean knows his Persephone from his Proserpina."

Tyler grinned. She looked like the cat who ate the canary. Whether that was because of her not-so-subtle Dean mention or the fact she knew Persephone's Roman counterpart was Proserpina, Tyler wasn't sure.

"We clearly don't need Dean."

"He'd be too distracting? Like my—*gag*—brother?"

"Your future-brother-in-law is more my type."

"Than Dean?"

"Than your brother!"

She laughed. "And Dean?"

"Geez. What about him?" Tyler was uncomfortable with the direction of this conversation. *Dean, Dean, Dean.*

"He's a good guy."

"Is he?"

Hot? Yes. Nice? Question mark.

"Yes. And talented. You should see him when he teaches the figure drawing class at the community center. He's so in control and poised. He's enthusiastic about his students and respectful of the nude models. The way his hands move when he draws is masterful, and—"

"Okay, okay. Message received. Are you trying to set me up with Dean? Because I just got out of a relationship, and I'm not—"

"No, Tyler. I promise I'm not. Well, I kind of am, but mostly, I'm being nosy."

"I'm a disaster and haven't exactly been putting my best foot forward on this trip."

"You're a fantastic teacher and won a lot of money on TV by being smart. Sometimes life is a disaster. People will either accept you for your mess, or they don't deserve you."

Tyler's cheeks went hot. "Thanks, Rosie. And thanks for inviting me. I needed this."

"Hey!" Leo yelled from up the road. Rosie and Tyler both snapped to attention. Leo was standing on a big boulder right at the curve of the road. On one side of the street, there was a sharp drop into the lake. On the other, there was a small shoulder and a quick ascent up the mountain, making the road feel incredibly narrow. "Come check this out! You can see Skipper Glacier from here!"

A childlike excitement blistered through Tyler. He'd never seen a glacier in person. He took a quick step forward and promptly slipped in that awful silt again, landing hard on his butt and tweaking his knee.

"Oh, fucking perfect," he groaned.

Then came the rain.

Chapter Six

DEAN REALIZED VERY QUICKLY that his winter coat was not waterproof. He and Tyler made quite the pair—Tyler shivering and covered in that gray mud again and Dean shivering and soaked through from the cold rain.

They could see the town in the distance, lit up and cozy-looking. Skipper Glacier, which was on the other side of the lake, was visible once you skirted around the edge of the mountain. It fed into Skipper Lake, leaving large icebergs that rose from the frozen water.

Leo was practically having an orgasm about the otherworldly blue crevasses in the glacier. He would be chasing the color all over the place in his next art collection. As they oohed and ahhed over the view, the glacier calved, causing cracks of ice to build up at the base.

Dean whooped in shock at the sight, adrenaline pumping. It almost helped him forget how miserably wet he was.

He wished that seeing such beauty inspired him to

draw, but he never captured the magic with his pencils that he saw with his eyes. His work always disappointed him. He could have drawn that glacier a million times, and it would never live up to the view in person. He had all the technical skills but none of the creativity.

"Should we keep going into town?" Rosie asked. She seemed unaffected by the rain, her eyes full of the wanderlust Dean had so often seen in Leo's.

"Where did those boulders come from?" Tyler asked abruptly, not answering her question. He was staring at the mountain.

There was a mix of snow, rock, and dirt toward the bottom of the slope with a denser slab of snow toward the top. The tips of evergreen trees peeked through the thick blanket.

"Presumably, up there," Dean said.

"And how deep do you think that snow is?" Tyler asked.

"Really fucking deep."

"Yeah. It covers those trees."

Tendrils of uneasiness spread over Dean's shoulders.

"It's awesome," Leo said. Everything was awesome to Leo. He was golden and loved and talented.

"Yeah." Dean took a shaky breath. It was terrifying.

"I'm going to head back to the cabin," Tyler said, his voice full-on Eeyore. "I'm covered in mud. Again."

"I'll go with you. I'm soaked," Dean said. He felt funny. Something wasn't quite right. "You two go on ahead. Get lunch, wait out the rain."

Rosie and Leo put up some mild resistance, but within

minutes, Tyler and Dean were walking back to the cabin together, and Rosie and Leo were heading into an adventure, happy as clams.

"So… teaching," Dean said after too many minutes of silence.

"Yep. What about it?"

"Well, we both do it. I thought it would be a good conversation starter."

Tyler nodded but didn't say anything.

So it obviously wasn't that good a conversation starter.

"What do you want to talk about?" Dean asked. The steady patter of rain against Dean's face and body was driving him out of his skin. He needed a distraction.

"Do we have to talk?" Tyler asked, which was so anti-social and grumpy it made Dean smile.

"Yes."

"Okay. Sports, then." Tyler waved his hand like the topic didn't matter one bit.

The rain picked up. It was loud enough that Dean had to yell. "Veto."

Tyler huffed. The rain had darkened his hair under his hat, and it stuck to his neck and cheeks. His cheeks were pink from the cold.

"Here. Hold on." Dean halted Tyler with a hand on his arm.

"You want to stop?"

"No, just…" Dean gently removed Tyler's beanie. It was sopping wet and surely hurting more than helping. Tyler's eyes widened. "You have a hood." Dean flicked Tyler's hood over his head, sending a spray of water droplets everywhere. It was wet on the inside, but it would be better than the hat.

"Oh." Tyler blinked several times. "Thanks. We're almost back."

"Yeah. We should keep moving."

They eyed each other. Tyler kept opening his mouth and shaking his head, like he had a million things to say.

"What?" Dean asked.

Tyler shook his head. "So last night… I, um. Fuck, I'm bad at this. I saw—"

A low, distant rumble cut him off.

"What's that noise?" Dean asked, his heart jumping into his throat.

"I don't know."

The sound lasted all of thirty seconds but seemed longer. He felt the rumble in his bones. They both froze to listen, but there was no visible source.

"Oh God. Look at that." Dean pointed to the lake beside them. There were low waves rolling under the thin ice, breaking it up into jagged puzzle pieces.

"Do you think the glacier calving could cause waves like that?" Tyler asked.

Dread filled Dean's chest. "No. I think that was something much different."

Tyler scrambled to keep up with Dean as he marched back the way they'd come.

"Where are you going?" Tyler asked. His feet slipped

in the godforsaken mud. His snow boots had zero traction, which was what he got for picking ones that were trendy rather than functional.

Dean was frantically calling someone on his phone. "Pick up, pick up, pick up. My service sucks."

"Dean, slow down."

Dean didn't listen. He took off at a jog. "Do you have any bars? Call Rosie," he shouted back to Tyler. "See if she picks up."

Tyler couldn't run and use his phone at the same time. Hell, he hadn't run since high school gym. He worked out by riding his bike to school.

Tyler found Rosie's number and dialed. It rang a few times before Rosie answered breathlessly. "Are you guys okay?" she asked.

"Yeah. Why? Are you?"

"Yes. We were in town when we heard it. Everyone here is freaking out."

Dean made it to the curve in the road, where they'd turned around earlier, and came to a dead stop. Tyler caught up, and everything fell into place then.

The rumble. The waves in the ice on the lake.

Slushy mud and snow covered the road. It looked like someone had poured a giant, frothy Frappuccino down the mountain slope and into the lake. They couldn't see the other side of the road, and the pile was dotted with rocks and boulders and upside-down trees. It was higher than their heads.

"Holy shit," Tyler gasped.

"Are they okay?" Dean asked.

"Yeah. They're in town." Tyler put Rosie on speakerphone. "We were standing right here fifteen minutes ago." Sourness rumbled through Tyler's stomach, and he thought for one embarrassing moment that he might throw up.

Dean grabbed his shoulder. Maybe to steady himself. Maybe to shore up Tyler and keep him from puking. "We're okay, though. And they're okay. So it's okay."

"Stop saying *okay*," Tyler mumbled, but it was half-hearted. They were separated from their friends by a fucking avalanche. Nothing about this situation was *okay*.

"This doesn't look too bad," Dean said, but that was blatantly false. It looked horrible. "How long will it take to clear it? A day?"

A whole day? A day with Dean Humphries and no buffer? Images of Dean on his knees last night bombarded Tyler.

"It sounds like no one was hurt. We were the last people in that spot. I'm going to call Brooks," Rosie said. "Maybe she can give us an idea of what we're working with here."

They said their goodbyes, and she hung up. Tyler and Dean waited in silence for her call back.

Dean still had his hand on Tyler's shoulder, a reassuring weight that Tyler didn't want to admit was helping.

Dean hadn't turned away from the huge mass of snow and mud. "Do you think we're safe here? Could there be another one?"

They were far back from the terminus of the avalanche, but Tyler suspected the slide and the persistent rain had weakened the remaining blankets of snow on the slope.

"No idea. Let's move. No reason to risk it."

Tyler grabbed Dean's hand, and they hurried back toward their cabin. They were both wearing gloves—wet gloves due to the rain that had yet to lighten up—but Tyler imagined that Dean's skin was warm. He imagined Dean as a lifeguard pulling him to safety. He did everything in his power to *not* think about a terrifying sheet of snow and mud coming toward them. They reached their driveway in no time at all.

The Chum Smoke Cabins were located in a meadow alcove. The slopes of the surrounding mountains were no longer directly beside them. The sight of their cabin seemed to pull Dean out of whatever daze he'd been in since they'd heard the avalanche. He freed his hand from Tyler's.

As they reached the porch of their cabin, a huge gray dog bounded out of the woods and straight toward them.

Tyler shrieked at the sudden appearance, a testament to how jumpy he was.

A man on skis appeared directly behind the dog.

"Oh good, you guys are here. Brooks said she saw you walking into town this morning," the man said.

"Wrangell?" Tyler asked. The man was familiar, but as he moved out of the trees and snapped his skis off, Tyler noticed an unruly beard and a manbun. So he wasn't Wrangell, who had been clean-shaven the night before.

"You know him?" Dean said.

"No," the man said, talking over them. "Wrong triplet."

"Triplets. Wow." Tyler hadn't realized. "You must be Sarg? Wrangell was searching for you last night."

The man whistled to his big dog, who trotted over and plopped down at his feet. "Yeah, well, he didn't find me. He never does. He should have sent Brooks. Now they're both stuck on the other side of that big, ugly slush flow. I'm Sargent, but don't call me that." He patted the dog's head. "This is Iceworm."

"Wait, wait," Dean said. "Slow down. You and Brooks and—"

"Wrangell," Tyler provided helpfully.

"Right. You're triplets?"

"It's not that interesting," Sarg said mildly.

"What did you call the avalanche? A slush flow?" Tyler asked. "We just saw it on the road. Our friends are stuck on the other side."

"Yeah. They happen during breakup season when the snow starts to melt and we get big rains, but we've never had one hit the road. Brooks asked me to check on you." Sarg's eyes lingered on Tyler, probably noting how utterly unprepared he was for Alaska. "You look safe and sound to me."

"We're fine," Dean said, his melodic voice abnormally harsh. "Our friends are in town, though."

The dog, Iceworm, padded over and bumped his head against Tyler's leg, getting mud from Tyler's pants on his snout.

"Well, no worries then. You're well out of avalanche

danger here at the cabin, and the town is as well. It'll only be four or five days until you'll see your friends again. Not bad for this part of Alaska."

"What?" Dean and Tyler both said in alarm at the same time.

Tyler's vision went wonky. "What do you mean four or five days?"

"It will take that long to clear the road. Which is pretty quick for remote Alaska. You're lucky we're on the road system, or it would be longer."

"We're stranded here. Without them?" Dean said.

Sarg smiled, and it transformed his rugged face completely. "Or you could look at it the other way around. They're stranded there without you. You could drive back to Anchorage if you wanted. You're getting the better deal. You have your luggage, a sauna, a hot tub, your vehicle. And each other."

Chapter Seven

THEY SAID their goodbyes to Sarg and Iceworm, who disappeared into the woods like Alaskan apparitions, and went inside.

Dean refused believe that man. Sargent. *Sarg.*

Four or five days! That was ludicrous.

Tyler made a beeline for the bathroom. He was stripping off his outerwear, which Dean had forgotten was covered in mud.

"Should I get you some clothes?" Dean asked Tyler through the door to the bathroom. If they were going to be stuck together for some unknowable amount of time, then Dean needed to be nice.

"Uh. Sure," Tyler said.

Dean took off his own wet coat and wet jeans, which were a very silly choice for this type of weather. He changed into a pair of gray sweats and a T-shirt. He found the aqua sweatpants Tyler had worn to bed and grabbed him a random tropical shirt from the top of his duffel bag.

He knocked on the bathroom door, and Tyler opened it.

A lot of things had thrown Dean for a loop that day, but Tyler in nothing but plaid boxers topped the list. Dean didn't understand why exactly. He had seen it all the day before. But Tyler's hair was wet from the rain, and it had started to curl into angelic ringlets around his face. His legs were pale and vulnerable-looking, and he had a large, red birthmark that stretched across his left knee and down his calf. His body was solid with an appealing layer of fat that made Dean want to grab on.

"Dean."

"What? Oh, right." Dean handed the clothes over.

Tyler's phone rang, and he dove for it before putting it on speaker so they could both hear. Rosie was on the other line.

Rosie and Leo had gotten a room at a restaurant and hotel called Dog Salmon Saloon, and townsfolk were telling them to settle in for the long haul.

His friends were getting an adventure, and they would take it in stride. They were undoubtedly only sad to not have their luggage full of sex toys with them.

Tyler idly scratched his bare stomach, and Dean had to tear his gaze away. "I'm going to shower," Dean blurted, interrupting Rosie as she gushed about the halibut she'd ordered for lunch. "I want to warm up." It was roasting in the cabin, but the bathroom was the only place he could easily get privacy without being rude.

"Oh, of course," Tyler said. He was standing at the sink, mostly naked, but quickly got dressed and moved out of the way.

"You should try the sauna to warm up," Rosie suggested. "Take advantage of the amenities we're missing out on."

Dean met Tyler's eyes. A sauna with Tyler sounded simultaneously heavenly and torturous.

"That's a good idea," Tyler said. "Might as well make the best of a shit sandwich."

Tyler had never been in a sauna, and he wasn't impressed. He had sweat beading on his nose and pooling at the backs of his knees. And the air felt dry, not steamy like he'd expected. Maybe they had done something wrong.

The sauna had a wood stove and one dim light. It would have been romantic if not for the sweat.

Dean, wearing short swim trunks that showed off half a floral thigh tattoo, had a towel wrapped over his shoulders and hadn't opened his eyes in five minutes. He was on the bench directly across from Tyler, and their knees were almost touching. Tyler was pretty sure Dean was asleep, so he didn't even have enjoyable company with which to share the unpleasant experience.

And speaking of sleep, where would they both sleep? Not in the same room. This was not an only-one-bed situation. They were stuck together in a cabin that was more than big enough for two people, but it felt like an imposition to take over Rosie and Leo's bedroom. Their bags were still up there.

Tyler assumed Dean would have fewer qualms about invading their space considering he was seemingly in the habit of… invading their space.

"Why did you and your boyfriend break up?" Tyler blurted, and Dean didn't react.

"Incompatible expectations," Dean murmured.

"Did I wake you up?"

"No."

Okay then. Dean was just closing himself off from Tyler. Probably because he didn't want to talk. Tyler could understand that. He hadn't wanted to talk earlier, but since then, he'd been front seat to an avalanche, and his whole body felt full of bees.

"What expectations were incompatible?" Tyler asked. "Like monogamy expectations or views of the future?"

Dean opened his eyes, and Tyler felt like he'd stirred a lion from a deep slumber. It was exciting.

No. *Not* exciting. That was ridiculous.

It was annoying.

"Monogamy? That's your topic of choice?" Dean said. He had a knowing smile on his handsome face, so Tyler clearly hadn't hidden his curiosity about Dean's relationship with Leo and Rosie.

"I asked about your breakup."

"It's not that interesting. Viggo wanted me to be a different man than I am. We parted amicably because neither one of us cared that much."

"A year is a long time to spend together if you don't care."

"That's true."

"Is that common for you?"

"What?" Dean asked. "Caring?"

"Not caring."

"Busted." Dean sat forward, and Tyler realized how very close they were in the small sauna. "Why did you and your man break up?"

"He's not my man." It was humiliating to think about his relationship with Francis. Tyler had been such a fool.

"Noted. So tell me why?"

"He…" Tyler picked at the hem of his T-shirt. Dean's focus was too intense. "He stole from me. Drained my emergency fund." Granted, Francis had paid it back via a loan from his parents, but Tyler wasn't sure he would have done so if he hadn't gotten caught. It had been violating and made Tyler feel vulnerable in a way he'd never experienced. Realizing he was such a bad read of character had turned his world upside down.

Silence dragged out between them. A trickle of sweat rolled down his spine, and he twitched.

A hand landed on his knee. Tyler jumped.

"That sucks. I'm sorry," Dean said.

"Thanks. And no one should want you to be different than you are, Dean." Tyler needed to bring the conversation back around to Dean and take the scrutiny off himself.

Dean's expression seemed to tell a whole epic poem in

less than ten seconds, but Tyler didn't comprehend a word of it.

"Leo says I don't let people in," Dean said finally. "It's probably true. Or maybe people expect depth from me when I'm actually quite shallow."

Tyler smiled. "It's your face. It looks contemplative like a poet's."

"Is that a compliment?" Dean asked, a bit of teasing in his voice.

"No. Have you ever met a poet? They're so *ardent*."

Dean laughed. "Artists are the same. Leo is—" Dean shook his head, and Tyler wanted Dean to finish that sentence so badly. "Leo has so many *feelings*."

"Feelings are the worst."

"They really are."

Laughter bubbled up in Tyler's chest, but he shoved it down. "Fuck feelings."

"For real. Fuck relationships. Fuck expectations, and fuck—"

"Thieves."

"Well, that's obvious," Dean said. He moved onto the bench beside Tyler, and Tyler's pulse went haywire.

"Fuck avalanches," Tyler said, his mouth dry. It was so hot in the sauna.

"Yes, that. Fuck Alaska."

"Agreed. It's too pretty." Tyler was breathless. Maybe it was heat stroke. "It's pretty, and it tried to kill us."

That sucked the levity out of the room. The curved ceiling suddenly felt too close.

"Don't think about it. That's my plan," Dean said brashly. "Avoidance. It's healthy."

"Hard to think of anything else."

"Where's the weirdest place you've ever had sex?"

"What?" Tyler exclaimed, his voice echoing around the cedar-lined room. "Are you enjoying this? The sauna? Because I'm not."

"It's supposed to be cleansing. Answer me. Humor me."

If Tyler had thought Dean seemed like a lion earlier, it was nothing compared to the slumberous, prowling purr in his voice now.

"You first."

"A laser tag game."

"Oh. Wow. Okay. That's… interesting. Who with?"

"Leo." Dean studied Tyler for an extended beat. "Well, and Robin Erco and Wren Rebello and a few strangers. It was during the between time."

"What's the between time?" Tyler had so many questions.

"The time between when Leo and Rosie dated in high school and when they reconnected after her divorce."

"Why did you tell me it was 'during the between time?'" Tyler asked. "Why does that matter?"

A furrow appeared between Dean's eyebrows. "I didn't want you to think Leo had cheated. It was before they were together."

"But don't you all—" Tyler stopped. He was adult enough to understand that couples had rules and agreements about sex, and he needed to keep his mouth shut.

"Leo doesn't fool around with other people unless Rosie is involved too," Dean said, answering the question Tyler couldn't ask. "And vice versa. Did you see us fucking on the balcony last night?"

Tyler was shocked at the frankness but managed to give a quick nod. He didn't want to get into that. He felt embarrassed and inexperienced enough. "Yep. Sorry. I didn't mean to spy. It was an accident. So how did you have sex during laser tag?"

The quick bypass of the balcony conversation seemed to turn a lot of wheels in Dean's brain. Tyler hated the tense silence.

"Mainly with my mouth. I'm good at that," Dean said, his voice gruff. "And you don't have anything to apologize for. We were practically begging to be seen by doing it out in the open."

Tyler's body was betraying him. The sex talk. The way Dean was staring.

"A kitchen. That's my weirdest. An old ex's kitchen. Years ago." They'd been trying to spice things up, and it had seemed very naughty. To Tyler at least.

"That's not weird at all," Dean said.

"Maybe not for you!"

"You need some depraved friends to corrupt you," Dean said. "Someone to take you to the weird places."

Yes. That sounded… Wow.

"I don't think so," Tyler said. "I… I'm probably fine. I'm not really… you know…"

"I don't know. You're not really *what*?" Dean said. His

voice was so low that Tyler leaned toward him to hear him better.

"Adventurous."

"What's your kinkiest fantasy?" Dean asked. He had that boyish smile on his face. The one that felt like a tease.

"I don't have one." Which was bullshit, but his fantasies certainly had nothing on Dean's real-life experience.

"Liar," Dean said. "What's the best sex you've ever had?" Dean's focus was on him alone. It pinned Tyler in place.

"That's private." And he had no idea. It was all… just okay. He craved sex, but it never quite lived up to the hype in his head.

Dean gave a conciliatory nod. "Fair."

"What's the best sex you've ever had?" Tyler asked in return, feeling bold for posing such a question.

"Man, nothing compares to receiving that first ever blowjob, right? Simple. Vulgar. Fast because you've never felt anything so good. A little messy. Or a lot messy maybe. Do you like it messy?"

Tyler's head spun. It was so hot in the sauna, and he was so close to Dean. They'd drifted toward each other without Tyler realizing. There were only a handful of inches to cross, and they would be kissing.

He wanted that. He was pretty sure he wanted that. Mostly sure.

Dean must have read his hesitation because he put a hand on Tyler's chest before Tyler built up the nerve to lean in. "Hmm. Better not."

Tyler scooted back, putting distance between them again. His heartbeat was pounding in his ears, in his temples. He pointed at Dean. "That was fucked up."

"Yeah. Sorry. You just seemed—"

Tyler shook his head sharply, cutting Dean off. A drop of sweat slipped from Tyler's hairline and down his cheek. He wiped it away and was worried that it had looked like he'd swiped at a tear.

Without a word, Tyler scrambled off the bench, out the door, and away from the asshole in the sauna.

Chapter Eight

DEAN FOLLOWED Tyler into the house. He could hear Rosie's recriminations in his ear. He needed to be nice. To be gentle. To not take advantage of a guy who was hurting and anxious and had trust issues as tall as the mountains surrounding them.

Sex after almost being smooshed by an avalanche was not a healthy coping mechanism.

Tyler was scraping through his duffel bag and didn't react to Dean's appearance.

"What are you looking for?" Dean asked.

"A book. I thought I brought it with me. It's…"

"It's what?"

"Important to me. I brought my important ones so they wouldn't disappear when Francis moved out of my condo." He held up a thick paperback. "Found it."

Letting a guy who stole money from you move out of your house without supervision sounded unwise, but Dean wasn't going to say that.

"Is there a risk your stuff will disappear?"

"Of course. But Francis isn't a bad guy. He got behind on his—it doesn't matter. I had to get out of there, and it felt more important to be away from him than for me to be there protecting a bunch of junk. But I didn't want anything to happen to my books."

"Your trivia books," he said.

"Well, this one's about social strategy and reality TV, but yes."

"Why is a book about social strategy important to you?"

"I like games. Strategy games. Trivia. Games of chance." Tyler sat on the bed and frowned at him. "But I didn't love that stupid mind game you played in the sauna."

"That wasn't a game."

"Felt like one. Pretty sure I lost."

Dean sighed and weighed his options. He had wanted to kiss Tyler. He'd wanted to muss up Tyler's hair and yank him into his lap. To lick the sweat off his neck. To pull out the wild child underneath.

But Tyler had an earnestness that plucked at all the protectiveness deep in Dean's soul. He didn't sleep with people who were easily hurt.

"What is it that *you* want, Tyler?" Dean asked. If Tyler said no-strings fun, it would be incredibly hard to deny him. Dean usually tried to do the right thing, but it was hard when the wrong thing was way more fun.

"To spend the rest of my spring break reading and watching TV. I don't want to think about my breakup or my job or any of the things that keep going wrong. I want you to sleep upstairs so we both have our own space. And stop fucking with me just because I find you attractive. I'm not a plaything."

"You find me attractive?"

Tyler let out an exasperated laugh. "Don't get a big head. You're tall, which is basically the same thing in my lizard brain."

"You're, you know, hot too."

"Oh." It was clear Tyler wasn't used to compliments, even awkwardly delivered ones. He frowned down at his lap. "Thanks."

"But you recently went through a breakup."

"Which I don't want to think about. And so did you."

Dean pretended to zip his lips and throw away the key. "Noted. I don't want to lead you on. That's why I stopped you."

A weird expression flitted across Tyler's face. "Trying to kiss you *one time* wasn't exactly a marriage proposal, Dean. You're not…"

"I'm not what?" Dean had a sneaking suspicion Tyler had planned to say *relationship material*. Which was the truth, or so he'd been told many times before. He'd tried with Viggo because he thought that was what he was supposed to do at his age. It was what his friends seemed to be doing—pairing up and adopting dogs and having kids. But it had just proved he was still a failure at all things of the heart. You couldn't force love.

Surface-level guy—that was Dean.

Tyler shook his head, bringing Dean's attention back

around. "I wasn't expecting you to give me your letterman jacket. We're here without Rosie and Leo for who knows how long. Our only other company might be the Alaskan mountain man who appears randomly in the woods with his huge dog. I figured *why not*."

An unwitting laugh escaped Dean. "Kissing me to stave off boredom. Got it. I've been kissed for worse reasons."

A smile curled the corners of Tyler's mouth. Dean was mad that he'd missed his chance to taste those lips, but he'd made the correct decision. Now that they'd had a moment to reset, Tyler had asked for space, not a hookup.

"Can you put some clothes on?" Tyler said, snarky acid in his voice. He waved his hand in Dean's direction, indicating the whole of him in one sweep of his arm. "You're kind of the worst."

"Sure thing."

Dean grabbed his bag and dragged it upstairs to Rosie and Leo's room. It took him a full ten minutes to stop smiling.

Later that evening, after eating peanut butter and jelly sandwiches for lunch and dinner, Tyler disconnected from his laptop for long enough to pour them both a glass of wine. He'd been buried in the computer all day, watching a dating show with his headphones in, and Dean wasn't complaining. He'd needed the breather too.

Dean fiddled with the edges of his drawing pad, and snuck another secret look at Tyler's hands. Dean sucked at drawing hands, and he was only sketching Tyler's because they were right there, and that was better than trying to do his own. Tyler's fingers were blunt, and he bit his nails.

"Have you heard from Rosie and Leo?" Tyler asked him as he handed over a plastic wine glass full of a generous helping of white wine. It was their second each.

They'd hardly said a word to each other in hours, and Tyler's voice sent a delightful thrill up Dean's spine. The wine was going to Dean's head.

"Some texts. What about you?"

Tyler shook his head. "I had to turn off my phone. Francis keeps calling."

"Asshole. Well, Rosie and Leo are taking this whole thing in stride."

"They would," Tyler said darkly, and Dean willed himself not to laugh. "Did you know slush flow avalanches can happen on slopes that are only three- or four-degree grades? That's effectively flat."

"How did you learn that?"

"I looked it up." Tyler shrugged.

Dean drew the slope of a shoulder in one sweep, thinking back to Tyler standing at the bathroom sink, to him sitting slightly hunched and uncomfortable and sweating through a T-shirt in the sauna.

"Tell me more."

"There was a famous one in Norway in the 1950s."

Dean flipped the page of his sketch pad as Tyler regaled him with avalanche trivia. Dean tried to conjure up images of the last model to pose for his class at the community center. Her legs had been short and strong, and she'd had an old tattoo on her ankle, but as he started drawing a thigh, his mind fought the impulse to shade in a birthmark.

"What are you drawing?" Tyler asked, sitting up from his slump on the sofa to see.

Dean closed his book with a decisive snap. "Nothing."

Chapter Nine

TYLER WAS PERFECTLY content being a lazy bum. He was *go, go, go* during the school year and had learned to take full advantage of every precious break. So he was happy eating simple food, reading his books, and watching his shows.

Dean, on the other hand, was pacing the cabin like an agitated wolf within twenty-four hours. He'd spent the morning taking inventory of their supplies as if they were stranded in an apocalypse. Rosie and Leo and the town of Silverbrite Springs were the ones who were cut off from the world, not them. Tyler's helpful input—"If we run out of food, we have a vehicle and can literally drive back to Anchorage"—was met with a tic of a strong jaw and growling under Dean's breath.

Granted, Tyler wasn't trying to help Dean's restlessness. The cabin didn't have a TV, and Tyler had spent three hours with his headphones in completely absorbed by a show on his laptop about hot singles on an island. He could have offered to let Dean watch with him, but he hadn't.

Dean was bored, and Tyler was enjoying his frustration.

"Tell me about Francis," Dean asked, catching Tyler without his headphones in while returning from the bathroom.

"Absolutely not."

"Then go outside with me."

"Yes, because we've had so much luck out there so far," Tyler said sarcastically.

"We're in Alaska. Don't you want to see it? Experience it?"

"I've seen the northern lights, a glacier, and an avalanche. I'm good."

Dean plopped down beside Tyler on the sofa. "Tell me some random facts then. About anything. I love listening to you talk, and I'm going stir crazy here."

Tyler ignored the thrill that went up his spine. Francis had hated when Tyler would get on a roll about his interest of the hour. "It's only been a day. You can't have cabin fever yet."

"Let's get in the hot tub."

"No."

Dean went to his knees on the couch and faced Tyler. "I know what you're doing. Icing me out. I deserve it. But, Tyler"—Dean grabbed Tyler's hands and stared at him very seriously—"I am so bored."

Tyler couldn't stop his laugh, no matter how hard he tried. "Here. Draw my elbow or something. Like yesterday. I'm watching hot hotties on a beach right now." Dean tensed, and Tyler looked up in alarm. "What's wrong?"

"Nothing. I wasn't … yesterday. What are you talking about?" Dean shifted away from him.

"You were drawing me. Or parts of me. It's probably subconscious for you. I mean, you draw people for a living. I'm sure it's an instinct to sketch whatever body is in view."

Dean gaped in confusion, but Tyler had seen it with his own eyes.

"I'm going for a walk," Dean finally said.

"Okay."

"Don't wait up."

"It's not even dinnertime. If you're not back by nightfall, I'm contacting search and rescue, which would cost us a fortune, and neither of us make enough money for that."

"Fine." Dean got up and quickly bundled into his winter gear. His coat was damp from the day before, and Tyler felt a twinge of worry.

"Where are you walking?" Tyler asked. "It's cold out there." The temperature had dropped back below freezing that morning once the rain showers had passed. The ground was an ice rink.

"Wherever my feet lead me," Dean said, which sounded like the most irresponsible, woo-woo bullshit Tyler had ever heard.

"Have fun."

"I will."

"Say hi to Sarg for me if you see him."

"I will." Dean's voice was clipped.

"Bye."

Dean didn't say goodbye but just trudged outside on his own.

It only took thirty seconds for Tyler's overthinking to catch up with him. What if Dean got lost out there? What if he hurt himself and couldn't make it back to the cabin and died of hypothermia? What if there was another avalanche? What if Dean saw Sarg in the woods, and they fucked?

Okay, that last worry was less of a worry and more of a fantasy, but Tyler was enough of an anxious mess to not leave it up to chance.

He grabbed his coat, boots, and gloves and followed Dean outside. The sun was peeking through the gray clouds, sending sprays of light across the lake. Dean was nowhere to be seen.

Tyler tromped—carefully because he figured his next big wipeout would result in broken bones—down the driveway.

Dean wasn't on the road, but he was picking his way along the edge of the lake, heading in the opposite direction of Silverbrite Springs and the site of the avalanche.

"Wait up!" Tyler called down to him, but Dean either ignored him or didn't hear.

Tyler determined it would be faster to follow the road before heading down the bank to the lake. It didn't take that long to gain on Dean. The forest grew thicker, encroaching on the road. There were short trees on the lake side of the street. Willows, maybe, but it was hard to tell as they had no leaves.

He spotted Dean through the trees. He had stopped and had his phone out, pointing it at something Tyler couldn't see.

"What are you looking at?" Tyler whisper-shouted so Dean would hear him.

Dean jumped at his voice and flicked his gaze toward Tyler. Dean was holding himself very still, and alarm bells started ringing in Tyler's ears.

"Come here," Dean mouthed, so Tyler carefully pushed his way through an opening in the willows and down onto the bank of the lake. It was slick and rocky, but he made it without breaking a leg.

Once he was within reach, Dean snagged Tyler's elbow and pulled him into his side. He gently skimmed his fingers over Tyler's lips to tell him to be quiet, and Tyler's body lit up like a dance club.

Dean leaned in and whispered in his ear. "She's beautiful."

TYLER'S BREATH was coming fast, and Dean tried to ignore the way that conjured up images in his head he should not have been having. He'd pulled Tyler to him, but Tyler had ended up slightly in front. He smelled good, and Dean was so distracted by that he missed the moose lifting her head and stepping to the next tree.

They were about thirty yards from it. He was shocked

by how large the animal was. He'd assumed seeing a moose would be similar to spotting a deer in the wild, but it was not at all the same. The moose looked prehistoric and dangerous.

"That's a bull," Tyler whispered. "You said, 'She's beautiful,' but that's a male."

"It doesn't have antlers, though." Dean said, keeping his voice low.

"They fall off in the winter."

The moose dipped his head to the ground, and Dean saw that Tyler was right. There were circular bare spots above his eyes where antlers had once been.

The moose lumbered three steps closer, paying them no mind. He was solely focused on eating the thin branches of the shrubby trees along the road.

"Oh God," Tyler said softly. "Let's go." He tried to take a step backward but bumped into Dean.

"It's fine. He doesn't care about us."

At the sound of Dean's voice, the moose moved his big-ass snout and stared directly at them. His ears went back.

"Nope. Not fine," Tyler said. He was running up the slope, through the trees and toward the road before Dean could respond. Luckily, he grabbed Dean's hand and dragged him along.

They reached the gravel road in seconds, and the moose was barely visible through the brush. It huffed and charged by where they'd previously been standing before returning to his meal, seemingly docile as a dairy cow.

Dean's heartbeat was hammering in his ears. "Holy

shit." That had been exhilarating and terrifying, and Tyler had just saved his life!

"Fuck you, dude," Tyler growled, flinging Dean's hand away and marching back toward their cabin.

"Wait. Why are you mad at me?"

"Because!"

Dean hurried to catch up, but anger made Tyler quick. Dean had to jog, which was very difficult on the icy road

He managed to reach Tyler before the driveway to their cabin. He grabbed Tyler's elbow and spun him around, pinning him to the sturdy, rustic road sign pointing toward Silverbrite Springs. Tyler reached up to push him away, but Dean managed to catch his hands and restrain them against his own chest.

Dean felt out of control. He was angry that Tyler was angry at him. He was relieved that Tyler was okay, that Tyler had made sure Dean would be okay too. He was tired of fighting a fight that wasn't his to win. He was so confused by the landslide of feelings rushing through him.

He didn't do feelings. He wasn't used to having them. Not like this. Not in a way that overwhelmed him.

Tyler's hands curled into the fabric of Dean's coat and held on. His cheeks were flushed, and his eyes were so bright it looked like he'd been crying. But it was anger. All heat and fury and—

"Fuck you," Tyler whispered again.

"Thank you," Dean responded. He slipped his hands to Tyler's wrists, and Tyler yanked him a step closer. "Thank you."

Their noses brushed, and Tyler's harsh breath hit Dean's lips. He let go of one of Tyler's wrists and touched his cold cheek. When Tyler didn't stop him, he moved his hand to the slope of Tyler's throat, to his shoulder.

Tyler closed his eyes, his brow furrowed. Dean knocked Tyler's hat off as he combed his fingers through Tyler's amazing, messy hair. It caused Tyler to tip his head back, his lips parted.

Tyler's expression almost brought Dean to his knees. He was going to draw that face. That beautiful, fiery, fucking perfect face.

With no warning—or maybe with all the warning in the whole damn world—Tyler shoved him away.

Tyler glared at him. Dean was going to draw that face too.

"Better not," Tyler said, his voice a poisonous echo of Dean's the day before in the sauna.

Chapter Ten

TYLER WENT DIRECTLY to the bedroom and firmly shut the door behind him. He was so mad.

That almost-kiss had been the most erotic, and frankly most romantic, moment of his whole dang life. And Dean's recklessness, his gratefulness, his… everything about him infuriated Tyler.

How dare he almost kiss Tyler. Again!

That wishy-washy asshole.

Dean didn't let people in. He had been with a guy for a full year and didn't care that it had ended. He was feelingless!

Shit like kisses and sex and intimacy didn't mean anything to Dean. He'd made that very clear.

A lightbulb went off in Tyler's brain. It didn't mean anything.

It didn't *have to mean anything.*

He flung the door open. Dean was sitting on the sofa

with his head in his hands, and he jumped to his feet when he heard Tyler.

"No kissing," Tyler said. That was rule number one. Rules were great for an overthinker.

"Okay. I'm sorry. Tyler, I really—"

"We don't have to be friends. Or talk. In fact, it's better if we don't." Rule number two. Friendship would just complicate it.

"Hey, maybe I want to be friends with—"

"Do you have condoms? I haven't been tested in a while." Safety was rule number three.

Dean's mouth dropped open. "What's happening right now?"

Never mind. They could come back to that.

"It doesn't mean anything. No strings. Rule four."

Dean's gaze sharpened on him, and Tyler's pulse jumped. That intensity was scary and hot all at once.

"What are you asking me for, Tyler?" Dean said, his voice a sexy rumble.

"Not asking. Offering."

"Hmm. What are you offering then?"

Fuck, Dean's voice was the sexiest thing in the world. Tyler laughed at himself and panic-walked into the kitchen to get a drink.

Over his shoulder, he said, "Rebound sex. Obviously."

Dean caught him by surprise. A face-first into the refrigerator surprise.

Tyler gasped. He wanted to melt, to press back, to go pliant. But he had always been ruled more by his brain than his body, as much as he wished that wasn't the case. His brain was slower to jump on board.

"I'm on PrEP, have a good bill of health as of two months ago, and a dopp kit full of condoms," Dean said.

"Okay."

"Do I get to add rules to this arrangement? Or is this an autocracy?" Dean had Tyler pinned with his big, strong hands, and he added his mouth to the mix, placing a shiver-inducing kiss to the back of Tyler's neck. Then he replaced his mouth with a palm and pressed Tyler's face into the door of the refrigerator.

Tyler remembered the times he'd jerked off to Dean's hands and about lost control of his knees.

"You get a vote. Rebound sex can be democratic," Tyler gasped out.

"I vote for kissing."

Tyler tried to shake his head, but Dean was holding him too firmly. "Why?"

"Because I love kissing."

"Stalemate then. One against one. We need a compromise."

Dean licked the shell of Tyler's ear, and every muscle in Tyler's body liquefied. "Compromise is sexy."

"You can kiss me during the heat of the moment," Tyler gasped out. "During sex. Not outside it."

"Fair enough. I don't like it, though." Dean nipped the fleshy part of Tyler's earlobe. "I'm not sure this is a good idea, Tyler."

Tyler's hackles immediately went up. "I don't need any favors. I'm fine. If you're not interested, then—"

"Oh, I'm interested. And I'm gonna make you feel better than *fine.* I'm done doing the right thing. Bad ideas are sexy too."

That should not have turned Tyler on, but it did. He wanted to be bad for once.

"I'm the wrong thing?"

There was a heavy pause. "Yes. You're too innocent and sweet. Too… much heart."

Sweetness and heart hadn't served Tyler well in the past. They had made him an easy target.

"Do you usually muscle sweet guys face-first into appliances?"

"No. But I don't fuck them either."

"This doesn't feel like fucking," Tyler said, even though that was a big juicy lie.

"Yeah, it does." Dean slipped his hand from the back of Tyler's neck to his throat. "This okay?"

Tyler flung his head back onto Dean's shoulder on a gasp. "*Yes.*"

"You want to be muscled around. You want to fight."

"How can you tell?" Tyler asked earnestly. It *was* what he wanted, but he had never known how to ask for it.

"I just can. Am I right?" As Dean's lips traveled from Tyler's ear to his jaw, Dean went from holding Tyler against the fridge with his hands to pressing him against it with his body.

And that was all she wrote.

Tyler was done.

"Yes. *Yes.*"

It was a blur from there. Tyler was spun around,

pinned, pushed, kissed everywhere on his neck and shoulders and throat, and he somehow lost his shirt.

Tyler tried to take Dean's clothes off, but Dean harrumphed in the back of his throat and bit the naked sweep of Tyler's shoulder.

"Take off your shirt," Tyler whined.

"Not yet."

Tyler reached for Dean's sweatshirt again and promptly found his hands trapped above his head against the fridge.

"You're so goddamn pretty," Dean said.

"What? No one thinks I'm pretty."

Dean pressed their foreheads together. "You're out of breath. Your face is red. You keep moaning."

"I do?"

"Shush. You're sexy, Tyler. You have me itching for my pencils. I'd draw your O face and fuck myself to it every night, that's how pretty you are. Do you have to argue with me about everything?"

"You've never seen my O face. You might not like it."

"Oh my fucking God," Dean laughed. Then he practically threw Tyler to the floor.

Tyler tried to fight him on that too because that was what they both wanted. He tried to wiggle out of Dean's hold, to take control, to get away. And each time Dean put him back where he wanted him. Tyler hadn't realized wrestling could be sex, but each time his shoulder blades scraped against the wood floor, he lost his mind. Each time his socked feet scrabbled against Dean's denim-covered legs, then his bare feet against hairy legs as they both lost clothing, Tyler got harder and harder.

It was wild and playful and scary—but the fun type of scary. The top of a rollercoaster scary.

Once Dean's naked body was on full display, Tyler tried to slow his breathing and really look. Dean had the one tattoo on this inner thigh, which frankly was the best and sluttiest place for a tattoo, and he had dark, springy hair all over.

Hirsute—it jumped to the front of Tyler's mind like old SAT vocabulary.

"Damn." Tyler reached for Dean, but Dean flipped him onto his stomach.

"Be a good boy and stay there."

Tyler laughed. He waited a beat before trying to roll over.

"I'm fucking serious, Tyler."

Dean held the back of Tyler's neck into the floor with one hand and dragged his legs wide apart with the other.

Tyler froze. He could feel Dean's gaze.

"What are you going to do?" Tyler asked. His words were muffled by the hardwood.

It was the first time he had worried about logistics or positions. He'd been happy to let Dean muscle him into a stupor, trusting that Dean would eventually get him off in a satisfactory way.

Dean grabbed his ass. "I'm not sure yet," he whispered. His voice was rough. "I've got some ideas."

"Are you taking requests?"

"Do you have one?"

A slot machine of porn images spun behind Tyler's eyes. Of course he had requests. "Not really."

"I'll get you there, Tyler. If you trust me."

"I hardly know you."

Dean gave a long-suffering sigh, and Tyler tried to turn over again. Dean held him down none too gently.

Tyler loved the physical push and pull. He loved losing the wrestling match. He trusted Dean to give him an orgasm. But trust was more than physical. It was emotional.

He didn't trust Dean not to reject a kiss. He didn't trust Dean not to laugh when Tyler needed him to be understanding. Or not to say something that unintentionally hurt. He didn't trust Dean to let him in, to be vulnerable in turn.

Dean placed his lips on Tyler's shoulder blade. It was at odds with the hard way he was holding Tyler down.

"Pretty, pretty." Dean moved his mouth down Tyler's spine. "Pretty. You know what I thought when I first saw you on the plan?"

"*I hate that shirt. And every shirt he's worn since.*"

"No. I adore your shirts."

"*What a crybaby?*"

"No." Dean sat up and spread Tyler's ass cheeks apart. "I couldn't keep my eyes off you. I thought, *I want to know everything about him. I want to know what makes him tick.*" He licked up Tyler's crease. "I think I'm getting close, don't you?"

Dean's mouth felt so good. Too good. Tyler tried to

struggle away, but Dean didn't let him. "Pretty sure the answer to who I am isn't found in my asshole."

Another long beat. Tyler was learning to appreciate the breaks of silence. The moments where Dean was charging up, making up his mind, deciding on a next move or retort.

Finally, Dean chuckled. "I better check, just in case."

He started with his mouth. His tongue. The stubble on his chin. It was the most thorough rimming Tyler had ever experienced. He'd expected Dean to be acceptable at using his mouth. He'd witnessed it from down in the spruce trees, peering up at that balcony while Leo and Rosie and Dean went at it.

But this was next-level stuff.

"Stop squirming," Dean mumbled. "Stay put."

Tyler nodded, but his body had other ideas. His cock ached, and he couldn't help himself. He flexed his hips against the floor.

Dean smacked his ass. "I mean it."

The spanking resounded through the empty cabin, and the echo quickly warped to static noise in Tyler's ears. That sharp sting was glorious.

He'd had his butt slapped during sex before. But it was different with Dean. It wasn't harder or more painful. It had been playful, honestly. But Tyler's body suddenly felt like a Coke bottle that had been shaken up. He was trembling, and his skin was sizzling. The noise that escaped him was embarrassing and ten times too needy.

Dean flipped him onto his back. "Did I hurt you?"

"No." Tyler stared up at the pitched roof of the cabin.

"Was that okay?"

"Uh-huh." It was so okay that Tyler was done waiting. He reached for his cock. It wouldn't take much, two or three pumps at most. Maybe Dean would give him one of those sexy, aggravated, little huffs since Tyler was being so bad. And then he'd bust.

But he didn't get the chance. Dean grasped his wrist and squeezed.

"If you think I'm going to let you jerk off right now, you haven't been paying attention. Let *me* make you feel good."

"You are. You have."

"I've hardly started."

If that was Dean hardly starting, Tyler didn't think he could withstand him full throttle.

Dean grinned. "On your back or your stomach?"

"You're giving me a choice?" Tyler didn't want a choice. He wanted to be put in his place.

"Yes."

"Uh, back, I guess."

Dean grabbed Tyler's waist and flipped him onto his belly.

Tyler laughed, relief flowing through him. "Well, okay."

The mind games, the mental aspect of this, was turning him on as much as Dean's body and hands and mouth. Tyler couldn't remember that ever being the case.

His brain was usually the part of his body that he most had to fight in order to truly enjoy himself.

But this simple grab-ass with Dean was mixing and melding the physical and the cerebral, and it was the best Tyler had ever felt during sex. Which was *not good, not good, not good at all.*

It didn't mean anything. Rule three.

The avalanche would be cleared in a few days, and then Tyler would be the wallflower again. Forgotten, pushed to the edges, watching but not lucky enough to join.

"Hey. Focus." Dean rubbed a thumb over Tyler's taint.

"I *am.*"

"You think I can't tell that that big brain of yours is on the other side of the mountain by now?"

Tyler rolled his eyes. "I'd assume you're too distracted by my asshole to notice anything about my brain."

"Mmm. It is nice… You know, we can stop," Dean said. Everything slowed down. His hands gentled. He ran a fingertip from the arch of Tyler's foot to the back of his knee—the popliteal fossa, his brain unhelpfully provided, as if he were about to buzz in at trivia.

"I don't want to stop."

"Okay. I can be…"

"What?" Tyler asked.

"Sweeter? If you need me to be."

Tyler groaned. "Dean."

"Hmm?"

"Shut up and fuck me."

Another glorious, scary, wonderful silence.

"I'm not going to fuck you," Dean rasped darkly.

"Well, are you going to do anything besides stare?" Tyler thumped his forehead against the hardwood.

Dean didn't respond. Tyler heard Dean spitting, either into his hand or directly into his cock. It made Tyler tense and his whole body flush hotter than the nearby stove. He was embarrassed by how much spit as lube turned him on. It wasn't logical, and it didn't really work for him—he'd tried—but the *thought* of it was so dirty.

Dean crawled up Tyler's body, caging him in, and yanked Tyler's head to the side using his hair.

Tyler tried to duck his head out of Dean's hold, but Dean just fisted the hair harder.

"I'm gonna kiss you. And you're gonna let me, aren't you, Tyler?" He snaked his hand from Tyler's hair to the front of his throat, then lifted his face off the floor.

Tyler had to scramble to get his elbows underneath him. The change in position brought Dean's pelvis into contact with Tyler's ass. Dean's spit-slick cock slid between Tyler's cheeks.

"Oh God, will you please fuck me?" It was not fair that Dean had such a nice cock.

"No. I already told you." Dean thrust, and they both made noises—Tyler's hungry and Dean's gruff. "I'm gonna kiss you."

Chapter Eleven

"AS WE'VE ALREADY AGREED, fucking and kissing aren't mutually exclusive. And you're not doing either," Tyler griped, arguing for argument's sake.

Dean sucked on the hinge of Tyler's jaw and kept rolling his hips. Another greedy noise ripped out of Tyler's throat.

"What do you need?" Dean whispered in his ear.

"Kiss me already. Jesus. You keep saying you will, but you won't freaking do—"

Dean used his superior height to kiss Tyler over his shoulder. It was light. A barely there clinging of their lips.

Tyler was a sticky, shivering mess, and Dean was powerful and in control and using Tyler's body like his own personal fuck toy.

But the kiss.

Dean's starving mouth.

The slow sweep of his tongue.

Dean moaned and dug his fingers into Tyler's skin like he couldn't control himself.

Tyler had never been kissed with such intensity. It was scary and wonderful and… yeah, too much.

Tyler ripped his mouth away from Dean to gasp. "Please, stop. I need—"

"What do you need? Tell me," Dean demanded. His voice was a sexy, broken grumble, and Tyler could feel the slam of Dean's heartbeat against his back.

"I don't know. I want to come. I need more. Or less. I don't know." Tyler wasn't making sense.

"Harder or softer, angel?"

Fuck, fuck, fuck. He loved Dean's voice.

"I don't know. Just do something already!"

A small laugh escaped Dean. He bit the side of Tyler's neck, and Tyler's eyes rolled back.

"Anyone ever tell you that you're an incredibly difficult person?" Dean's voice was fond and tender, but those words tumbled over Tyler like sharp rocks.

He was not an easy person.

To rein in—according to his boss.

To handle—according to his mom.

To love—according to Francis.

It didn't matter how much Rosie pumped him up with words of affirmation. It didn't matter how many times Dean called him pretty.

The words he heard over and over again when he closed his eyes were the hurtful ones, and Dean had unwittingly stepped into that minefield.

Dean kissed his ear. "Don't."

"*Don't* what?"

"Don't let whatever ugliness just flitted through your brain hurt you. I love difficult."

Tyler's breath caught in his throat, and the pesky emotions he'd tried to avoid for a week burned behind his eyelids. He nodded, and Dean kissed his cheek.

"I can do this hard. I can flip you over, work my fingers inside you, and make you come. It will be rough and messy. Or I can do this soft. Kiss and suck and draw the come out of you like wisps of smoke. Your choice."

"Poetic," Tyler quipped, but his voice broke, still affected by his insecurities and Dean's swift, albeit temporary, victory over them.

"*Hard* it is." Dean was so steady and solid in the face of Tyler's ricocheting emotions and desires. So willing to ride them out and come out the other side.

Dean rolled Tyler over and immediately made good on his promises. He pushed Tyler's legs toward his chest, opening him up. Tyler hated this position, hated having his legs awkwardly up and frogged out, and that hatred turned him on more because Dean wasn't letting him squirm away.

Dean brought his fingers to Tyler's lips. "Suck… Fuck yes, like that."

Tyler got them as wet as possible. He knew neither of them were willing to get up and scrounge for lube, so spit would have to do, and he would need a lot of it.

Dean pressed the fingers inside fast. It was just on the right side of painful, and the moan Tyler let out startled them both.

"That's it, Tyler. No fighting now, huh?"

"No." Tyler dropped his legs onto Dean's shoulders.

Dean licked around his fingers, smoothing the way for more forceful thrusting.

"Tight," Dean murmured, his brow furrowing.

Tyler let out a strangled laugh. "What a porny thing to say."

Dean glanced up at him and curled his fingers hard. Tyler yelped and flailed as sensation shot from deep in his groin, radiating outward. He was close, he realized. All Dean would have to do was breathe on Tyler's cock for him to come.

"If I wasn't adamantly against being farther than three inches from your body, I'd go get a dildo. Fill you up. Then crawl up your body and fuck your chest until I bust on your face."

"*That.* I want that."

"I'm not leaving."

"The chest thing. I want that." He reached for Dean to drag him up there, his own pleasure all but forgotten.

But of course, Dean wasn't having that. He fucked Tyler hard with his fingers and grabbed his balls.

Tyler's head hitched back, and his fingers scrabbled against the wood floor.

"You like that?"

"Yes." Tyler was almost there.

"Give me your hand."

"Don't stop touching me."

"Give me your fucking hand."

Tyler lifted his hand toward Dean. Dean licked every finger, then spit in his palm.

"Jerk off."

"Yes, thank you, thank you." Tyler grabbed his dick, and Dean put his mouth back to Tyler's hole. It was a crowded maze down there, but nothing had ever felt so amazing.

Tyler jerked himself, and just as he was about to come, Dean squeezed his nuts.

"Harder." The word burst from Tyler's mouth without forethought.

Dean squeezed harder.

It hurt, and it was everything Tyler had ever desired. His orgasm cracked through him. He writhed. And he might have yelled. And Dean might have squeezed even harder, might have pegged his prostrate like it was a self-destruct button, might have done any number of wonderful, pleasurably painful things. But Tyler was sound and motion and sensation. He was oblivious to anything but the shock of good feelings shooting him to the rafters.

Eventually, his ears stopped ringing, his limbs stopped twitching, and he opened his eyes. Dean looked feral.

"You are so fucking precious. You know that, right?" Dean slipped his body up, up, up Tyler's.

"Huh?"

"A total delight. The absolute fucking best." Dean straddled Tyler's chest, pinned Tyler's hands above his head, and dragged his cock up the midline between Tyler's pecs. Tyler was sweaty and messy with come there, smoothing the way.

"What are you talk—"

"*Shh.* I'm having an orgasm here." Dean fucked against Tyler's chest with such power, it made Tyler breathless imagining the possibilities. He wanted that hardness, that force inside him.

"You are not."

Dean transferred Tyler's wrists to one hand and tightened his grip. He cupped his other hand over the top of his dick, pressing it harder to Tyler's chest and creating a tunnel for it to shuttle through.

"*Yet.* So close, though. I'm gonna draw your O face. Wasn't lying 'bout that. It was spectacular… And you taste good. Did I tell you that?"

Dean's words felt playful, but his voice was dead serious and his body was too, the slinging of his hips cocky.

"What in the world are you saying? I don't…" The veins in Dean's arm stood out in sharp relief, and his abdominal muscles tightened. "God, you're hot," Tyler blurted.

The first spurt of come hit Tyler's throat. The rest landed on his chin and lips.

Dean gasped. His brow crinkled, and his mouth dropped open.

Spectacular O face indeed.

They stared at each other for too long afterward, both gulping for air. Dean shuffled down and blanketed Tyler gently with his body.

Dean's mouth grazed Tyler's. Another soft brush of lips. A little slip of tongue.

Too much. Too good. And against the rules. Tyler ripped his mouth away and shook his head.

An emotion that almost looked like hurt rippled across Dean's face. It was there and gone before Tyler could say anything.

Dean rolled off. "A successful rebound adventure, yes?"

"Yes," Tyler said. That was an understatement.

"Cool. Let's do that a million more times. Get that evil ex all the way out of your system."

Chapter Twelve

DEAN HAD WANTED a bit of cuddling or quiet together time after the sex. But Tyler had stood up, showered, and gone to bed. By himself.

Which was fine. Dean didn't need a snuggle buddy to fall asleep with. He didn't need anything.

It wasn't that big of a deal. He was used to sleeping alone. Even when he and Viggo had tried to do the whole sleepover thing, Dean found himself unable to fully relax. He was usually uncomfortable sleeping next to other people. It was too intimate.

His first night of sleep with Tyler seemed to be the exception, but Dean was calling that a fluke.

So yeah, it was fine that he and Tyler had headed to separate bedrooms, separate beds. It was fine that all Tyler had given Dean was the equivalent of a *good game* once the sparkle of orgasm had worn off. They hadn't kissed afterward. It was one of Tyler's rules.

Which was… fine.

Rosie and Leo's bed smelled of Rosie's citrusy perfume, and Dean fidgeted for thirty minutes before he broke down and called Leo.

"Hello?" Leo answered, panting slightly. "Are you okay?"

"I'm *fine*. Are you okay? You sound winded."

"We're, well… we were—"

Dean laughed. "Gotcha. Why did you answer?"

"Because it's you."

Dean closed his eyes, touched by that. They had been friends a long time. Leo was one of the only people who had ever wormed himself deeper than the surface of Dean's life. Occasionally, Dean tried to insert some distance, but Leo never let it faze him. He always pushed back.

"Do you want to talk?" Leo asked.

Obviously, Dean wanted to talk. He'd called after all, but now he wasn't sure what to say. How to explain. And he was clearly interrupting.

"I don't know."

"Do you want to *listen*?" Leo asked, a seductive lilt in his voice that had never failed to draw Dean in.

"No. Thank you, though."

There was a long pause. Dean didn't turn down Leo and Rosie very often. In fact, he couldn't remember a single time he'd turned them down.

Leo didn't say anything, but Dean heard rustling on the other end of the line. "What are you doing?" Dean asked.

"Putting my pants on. If you're not going to listen to

us fuck, then you're going to talk about what's bothering you. Those are your choices, lover."

Dean sighed. "Okay."

"It's only me on the line," Leo said. "Rosie's going to shower."

"Okay."

"We can talk about it. Whatever's bothering you."

"Viggo didn't like you." Dean hadn't meant to say that. It had been a huge sticking point between them but wasn't the reason he felt so unmoored currently.

"Well, then. Good riddance."

"I don't think I liked *him* very much." Dean shook his head. "Why would I date a guy I didn't like? Especially for a year."

"Hmm." Leo considered that for longer than the topic deserved. "You want the soft truth or the hard truth?"

"What's the difference?"

"One might hurt."

"Soft truth, then," Dean said. "You're the pain slut, not me."

"It's a protective measure. If you don't like the person you're dating, then it's not hard when it ends. It's just… nothing."

"Yeah. That makes sense." And Leo was right. That hadn't hurt… too badly. Dean could have figured that out himself if he'd taken the time to navel gaze.

"One day, you're going to let someone see the things that make you special. Someone beside me."

That was slipping into hard truth territory, and Dean didn't appreciate it.

"There's nothing special about me," Dean said with a laugh. He was a mediocre artist, a decent art teacher, a superficial friend.

"There is. You have so much love in your heart, but you don't share it with anyone. I see it bottled up there. I see glimpses of it when we're together."

"How do I share my *quote unquote* heart? Is that a skill that every preschooler is taught, and I wasn't because my dad didn't hug me?" Dean joked.

Leo, of course, didn't take the bait. "Like every other skill, it takes practice. Maybe that's what you should do with Tyler while you're stuck together. Practice."

Dean's heartbeat quickly picked up, galloping in his chest. He hadn't brought up Tyler. Purposefully. It was like pressing on a bruise.

"I don't understand."

"It's low risk. He's not a potential love interest. You're both recently out of relationships, and neither of you are in a state to start another. So practice with the small stuff. Tell Tyler what you're thinking rather than censoring yourself. Practice showing your emotions. Maybe open your heart up to friendship. Real friendship, not the transactional, shallow friendship you have with most people."

"Hey."

"What?" Leo said. He sounded smug, and Dean was regretting making this call.

"That isn't small stuff to me."

"I know, Dean."

When Dean had almost kissed Tyler outside against the sign for Silverbrite Springs, he'd been showing every emotion, and it was awful. He'd been wide open and vulnerable, and it had terrified him.

And now Leo's suggestions were antithetical to Tyler's rules: they weren't friends, they didn't talk, and it didn't mean anything.

"It's worth it," Leo said.

"What is?"

"Love. Friendship."

"I know friendship is important." Dean was getting aggravated. "We've been friends for a long time. That's not nothing to me."

"Right, but Dean… one day, someone's going to put *you* first, and it'll blow your mind. And you'll want to put them first too. That's worth it. Worth the risk of getting hurt or getting rejected."

It wasn't rejection, per se, that scared Dean. He'd been turned down before. But exposing your weak spots and *then* being rejected?

No way. He wasn't doing that.

"If you say so," Dean said. "Tell me about Silverbrite Springs. What are the locals like?"

Leo let him change the subject. He regaled Dean with stories about the town that seemed to be nestled at the end of the earth. He talked about walking to a secret viewpoint of the glacier with Wrangell and Brooks, who were both stranded in town as well. He gushed about the locals' hospitality and gruff kindness.

And Dean listened with half an ear because he could hear Tyler moving around downstairs, and it was taking every inch of restraint in his body not to go down there and follow all Leo's suggestions.

Chapter Thirteen

"SO HOW'S THIS going to work?" Tyler asked Dean over breakfast the next morning.

"How's what going to work?" Dean grouched. He had hardly glanced up from his bagel, but Tyler wasn't going to let Dean's mood ruin his day.

Tyler often let other people's emotions affect him. He worried and fretted and thought every emotional change of wind was his fault. Francis had called him overly sensitive once. He'd thrown Tyler's empathy back in his face, accused him of being self-absorbed. Had said the world didn't revolve around Tyler. It was a lesson that had been simultaneously true and hurtful.

But Dean wasn't his boyfriend or friend, and it didn't matter if he was grumpy in the mornings. It wasn't a reflection on Tyler's worth.

"Our sex arrangement."

"So that wasn't a one-time thing?"

"Did you want it to be?" Tyler asked.

Dean set his bagel down, and his gaze traveled from Tyler's face down his body. "No. I told you that yesterday, that I want to do it a million times, which you responded to by leaving like I had the plague."

"Oh." A pinch of regret slipped through Tyler. "I'm sorry. Did that hurt your feelings?" Being lovey-dovey afterward had felt dangerous and contradictory to their arrangement.

Dean pressed his palms against his eyes. "It's fine. I'm fine. So let's talk about how this is going to work." He dropped his hands.

"Yeah."

"Well, if you want something from me, all you got to do is ask. Or better yet, show me."

Tyler swallowed hard. "Show you?"

"Yes. I'm a very visual person."

A small smile tickled Tyler's lips. "You're an artist."

"No. I'm not," Dean said. "Show me what you want."

"That's hard." Tyler stood up, though.

"I know it is. But I like difficult, remember?"

Tyler made his way around the table. Maybe, if he was brave enough, he could test out that fantasy that had been plinking around his brain for ages.

Without breaking eye contact, Tyler deliberately put his hands behind his back, trying to show without telling. He grasped his own wrists, so he was restrained.

"Okay. I see you," Dean whispered. He pushed Tyler to his knees. "Don't move your hands. Keep them right there unless you want me to stop."

Tyler had been on his knees for men before, but it felt

different with his hands locked behind his back. It felt different with Dean's dark eyes and beautiful, demanding voice. It felt different because this was so low pressure. Sex with Dean didn't mean anything, and that was incredibly freeing.

Dean took out his cock and stood up. "Look up at me."

Tyler reluctantly moved his focus from the dick in front of him and met Dean's eyes.

"You're gonna suck me. You okay with that?"

Tyler nodded. He'd never had strong opinions about cocksucking. It was okay—not great, not bad. He did it if his partner enjoyed it, but it wasn't an act he particularly craved.

But he was eager to get his mouth around Dean, to taste him, to be overwhelmed by him.

"If it's too much, push me away. Or tap my hip."

"Okay."

"Promise me," Dean said gruffly.

"I promise."

Dean threaded his fingers through Tyler's hair and pressed against Tyler's jaw with his thumbs, hinging it open. Dean slipped the tip of his cock into Tyler's mouth. Tyler did his best to lick it, but it was hard with no leverage. Dean had complete control, which was thrilling and daunting all at once.

"I like your hair," Dean murmured.

Dean slowly pressed his cock deeper, gradually testing Tyler's limits.

"And your smart mouth. I love your mouth. The

worst part of a blowjob is that you can't back talk me while you do it. Your voice, your mind... Fuck, you turn me on."

Tyler glanced up at Dean, whose whole focus was zeroed in on Tyler's face, his eyes. Tyler was suddenly unsure. He had expected Dean to fuck his throat, to use his mouth.

But that wasn't what this was, he realized. Dean was being... sweet. On purpose. Tyler started to shake his head, but Dean just tightened his hold and held Tyler immobile.

"Push me away if you want me to stop, angel."

Tyler almost did it. Almost released his wrists and shoved. He didn't want to hear Dean's praise. It didn't mean anything. It was pointless flowery language. Even the endearment—*angel*—was bullshit.

"You gave me control for a reason," Dean said. He finally thrust into Tyler's mouth. He was still being gentle, but at least it was *something*. "So let me use it how I want to use it."

Tyler rolled his eyes, and Dean laughed. Tyler held himself rigid, clenching his hands around his wrists, squeezing hard each time Dean spoke.

His jaw was aching, and Dean evidently had infinite sex stamina because he wasn't even breathing hard.

"I like you like this," Dean said after several minutes. "Unwelcoming. Challenging. But I can wait you out, Vlachos. I can wait until you're pliant for me. I love it when you fight, and I'll love it when you give in."

His last name and those not-so-nice adjectives—*unwel-*

coming, challenging—muttered with as much reverence as Tyler had ever heard, worked in ways that *angel* never would. Tyler fought it for as long as possible, fought the things that spilled from Dean's mouth, but eventually, his body took over. He relaxed into the tenderness, the unhurried drive of Dean's cock. Tyler's mind went fuzzy and soft-edged like a dream sequence in a movie.

A groan ripped out of Dean. "That's it. That's it, Tyler."

Dean slung his hips hard, his cock bumping Tyler's throat, slipping over his tongue, but Tyler didn't even gag. He just opened completely in a way that seemed to shock both of them. Dean came on a cry that Tyler barely heard through the static in his ears.

The cock in his mouth was replaced with Dean's lips and tongue before Tyler could react. His head was heavy on his neck, but Dean held his cheeks in his palms, held him up.

"You're wonderful. That was perfect," Dean murmured against Tyler's lips.

Dean kissed the hell out of him. A heart-swooping, heart-stopping kiss. Tyler's brain started to fight it, to fight how good that felt, but then Dean's hand was on his cock, and everything went blurry again. He gasped through the quick, sharp orgasm that Dean summoned from him in five seconds flat.

Then he was on his back, his hands and arms slack and spread out, no longer clenched behind him. Dean kissed Tyler through the aftershocks, mumbling compliments and praise and pressing their bodies together in an urgent, consuming way that melted Tyler's last functioning brain cells.

Chapter Fourteen

DEAN WASN'T sure if he'd taken Leo's suggestion or if he'd done the opposite. Tyler hadn't moved from his arms on the kitchen floor, so that was an improvement from the last time.

They were fully clothed; though Dean's T-shirt was come-splattered. He'd put his own cock away and pulled Tyler's sweats back up while he had still been out of it. Dean was working very hard not to kiss him.

"I've never had a threesome," Tyler said out of nowhere. His body was relaxed and slack against Dean, as if he wasn't in any hurry to move.

Thank God.

"Okay." Dean's brain spun through all the reasons Tyler might be bringing that up.

"I'm not a prude. I merely…" Tyler shook his head. "I have trouble getting into sex sometimes. And it seems exhausting to add another variable to the equation."

Oh boy. Dean had a million follow-up questions to

that little infodump. He lightly rubbed his cheek against the top of Tyler's head.

"It can be exhausting," Dean said honestly. He was sort of picky about group sex for that reason. "Lots of individual preferences, boundaries, and hang-ups to keep track of. That's not even accounting for emotions involved."

"But you do it."

"With the right people, yes."

"Like Rosie and Leo."

Dean felt the doors and shutters he used to protect himself slamming shut. He'd had this conversation with Viggo a few times, and it always resulted in jealousy and distrust.

"I've been friends with Leo a long time."

"Friends with benefits," Tyler clarified.

"Yes. Occasionally. Maybe not as often as you'd think. We understand each other's boundaries."

"That sounds nice."

Dean's shoulders were tensed, and he forcibly relaxed them. "Yeah?"

"You're lucky enough to have friends who understand you, and that understanding comes with affection. That's nice."

"It is. It's fun too. That's mostly why we do it. Because it's fun."

"Fun?" Tyler said. It was like he'd never heard the word in reference to sex before.

"Yeah, fun. You said you have trouble getting into sex sometimes?" Dean asked carefully.

Tyler turned his head and buried his face against Dean's neck. Dean's heart took off at a full sprint, and he tightened his arms, holding Tyler closer.

"Veto," Tyler whispered.

"Okay," Dean said immediately. If Tyler didn't want to talk about that, they would skip it, but the topic made Dean uneasy.

"How do *they* do it? Have sex with other people? Rosie and Leo. I've never considered having an arrangement like that, but it's …"

"What?"

Tyler seemed to weigh his words before sighing. "Intriguing, I guess? But how would I know if it's for me? How do you take that step to see if it's what you want? And what if it's not? How do you explain that you changed your mind? '*Oh, I'm sorry. I said we could blow other people, but then I got jealous?*'"

"That's exactly how you explain. Rosie and Leo have incredible communication. They check in with each other a lot. You should talk to Rosie about it."

"I'm talking to you about it, though."

Dean blew out a heavy breath. "I'm as single as you and not exactly a glowing example of good communication." Dean touched a lock of Tyler's hair. He twisted it around his finger. "For me, it depends on who I'm with. If they want an open relationship, I'll give that to them. If they want to fuck strangers together while on vacation, great."

"And if they don't want those things?"

"That's okay too. I don't have to have a Leo and

Rosie arrangement if that's not what works for the person I love, what works for our individual relationship."

"Whoa. Dropping the L-word."

"Leo?"

Tyler laughed at Dean's silly joke. "Okay, next question."

"Hit me. I'm enjoying the third degree. It's sexy." It was also against Tyler's rules, but Dean wasn't going to bring that to his attention. He wanted Tyler to break the rules.

"Why do you keep saying you're not an artist?"

It was on the tip of Dean's tongue to pull Tyler's move and veto, but the conversation with Leo tugged at him.

Practice. He needed to practice.

"Nothing ever measures up to what I see in my head," Dean said. It was hard to explain. "Artists like Leo make magic, but when I try, it's flat." *Uninspired.* That was what echoed in his head when he tried to create something beautiful. Uninspired and derivative. "I'm scared to try, maybe," he admitted, which was flinging all his doors and shutters wide fucking open. "It's easier to draw models in class. Less intense when there's separation there."

"I saw your sketches yesterday. Of my hands. My legs. They were so realistic. I can't draw anything but stick figures."

"I can draw form easily, and I could teach you. I'm a good teacher."

"Those who can't do, teach?" Tyler said, a smile in his voice.

Dean let his lips drift over Tyler's temple. "Exactly."

"I think you're too hard on yourself. Maybe you just don't see yourself—your art—clearly."

"Maybe."

"*Or* one day the right inspiration will come along, and it'll gobsmack you," Tyler said, which felt too close to truth for comfort. "You'll see a piglet dressed as a ladybug and have an epiphany. You'll become famous for drawing farm animals in costumes. The Anne Geddes of pigs."

"So my muse in that scenario would be pigs?"

"In costume! Piglets probably. They're cuter."

God, Dean loved the silly side of Tyler. His carefree laugh. His rapid-fire retorts. "I bet someone has already cornered that market."

"Bummer."

Dean hummed as if it truly were a bummer and let the topic pass on by. Tyler traced a line down Dean's abdomen, seemingly lost in thought or at least not sharing them.

After several minutes, Tyler said, "My brain and body aren't always in sync." It was an unusual echo to Dean's admission about his art. "My body will be full steam ahead, but my brain is off on a tangent, thinking about climate change or famous women authors or whatever. I can go through the motions, and it feels nice, but it doesn't feel as good as I want it to because my head is a mess. Does that make sense?"

Dean lifted Tyler's chin. "It does. It's better when your mind is engaged in the intimacy too." Tyler's return to the vetoed subject was exhilarating. Was that the push and pull of being open with someone? They were open in return?

Tyler smiled wryly. "That's true. But it's less intense when there's separation there. Between my brain and sex."

"It can be scary when those walls come down, huh?" Dean said.

"Yeah. I'm not sure if it's worth it. The exposure."

Dean rubbed his thumb over Tyler's eyebrow. It was slightly unruly, the blond hair poking up in the middle rather than lying flat. "We can practice."

"Practice what?" Tyler said, confused, and it made Dean feel like they'd been having two different conversations.

"Knocking the walls down. Correct me if I'm wrong, but fighting your brain, engaging it, was what made that blowjob so hot, right? I'm willing to fight you all fucking day."

Tyler suddenly looked cornered. "I made rules." There was a stubborn glint in his eyes.

"I'm not asking to break them."

Tyler sat up, and Dean could have punched himself in the face. Silence was freaking free. Tyler obviously wanted his walls up and firmly in place, and Dean's help was unwelcome.

"We're already breaking them, though. This was a whole conversation. While cuddling. And fuck." Tyler pinched the bridge of his nose. Dean rubbed his back because he couldn't help it.

"I have sex toys."

"What?" Tyler whipped around and stared down at Dean.

He shrugged. The conversation was killing him. He was going to yell at Leo when he got a chance. Opening up was torture. He felt like he'd been scraped face-first over cement.

"I'm changing the subject back to something easier. I have sex toys. I brought my favorites with me because I knew I might hook up with Rosie and Leo, and I only have so many hands."

"Okay." Tyler blinked, the wheels seeming to turn in his head.

"I'll show you… when you want me to show you. I'll make you feel good when you want me to make you feel good. I'll tie you up. I'll restrain you. I'll play those mind games you pretend to hate but actually love. And I'll follow your rules until you break them yourself. I'm yours to use until that avalanche is clear."

Dean nearly said that conversations and cuddling and kissing wouldn't change anything, that Tyler's boundaries were safe even if they snuggled a little, kissed a little, but Dean couldn't force the lie past his tongue.

Tyler's boundaries weren't safe, and neither were Dean's.

Chapter Fifteen

TYLER WAS EMBARRASSED to admit that his experience with sex toys began and ended with a dusty old dildo he'd had in his bedside table for eight years.

He'd never used it with a partner. Francis knew it was there. They'd talked about it since it lived next to Tyler's lube, but neither of them had been that interested in introducing it into the bedroom.

Tyler clambered out of Dean's arms. He didn't want to think about Francis. Or their sex life. Or the blaring foghorn in his head telling him he had been missing out on so, so much because he'd been too cautious, too conventional to be honest about his desires.

He really, really didn't want to think about the softness in Dean's eyes, the vulnerability, as they'd talked about art and sex and friendship. The conversation had felt special, as if Dean was letting him in on something that was secret and personal, which was *ludicrous*.

It was simply the result of the fantastic-sex hormones leaving their systems.

Tyler's chronic overthinking was not going to ruin the straightforward arrangement with Dean.

Sex. No strings. No feelings. With a deadline.

"I'm going to take a nap," Dean said. He was still sprawled out on the kitchen floor, looking like a pajama-clad sex god.

"It's not even lunchtime." They had only been awake for a few hours.

Dean took a deep, slow breath. And oh, Tyler was very familiar with exasperation. It often reared its ugly head whenever he missed social cues because his impulse to be a know-it-all was too great.

"Do you just want to get away from me?" Tyler asked. "You don't have to lie about taking a nap. We can be honest. I kind of want to get away from you too."

Dean sat up and laughed. He grabbed Tyler's hand and stared up at him with such an open, earnest expression. "I don't want to get away from you, but I'm happy to give you space. And I didn't sleep great last night."

"Why?" Tyler couldn't take his eyes off Dean's fingers wrapped around his own.

"Why what?"

"Why couldn't you sleep?"

"The ghosts of Rosie and Leo are strong up there."

Tyler was surprised by that. He'd assumed Dean had spent the night with them often enough that sleeping in their bed would have been no big deal.

"Oh. Well, if that's making you uncomfortable, you

could sleep"—Tyler almost said *with me* but stumbled on the words—"in the living room. Or we could see if Brooks would let us wash the bedding. She mentioned using her washer and dryer. If that's what's bothering you." Tyler's cheeks heated at the implications around dirty bedding.

His gaze wandered over Dean's plain black T-shirt. It was damp where Tyler had come all over it. Dean squeezed his fingers, and Tyler jerked their hands apart.

"You should nap. I should too," Tyler said faintly. Dean was watching him very closely. Everything was spiraling out of Tyler's control.

"Even though we just woke up?"

"Yep. But not together! We don't need to nap… together."

"Loud and clear, there, angel," Dean said, laughing.

"Why do you call me that?" Tyler asked. Dean held out his hand, obviously asking for help up, so Tyler assisted.

They had to stop touching, though. It was screwing with Tyler's brain. Luckily, Dean didn't hold on any longer than it took to get to his feet.

"I call you that because when I'm turning you on, you look shocked like an angel who's been corrupted." Dean advanced on him and lightly touched his cheek. "All innocent and pure, fighting your better nature." He dipped his head and brushed his lips over Tyler's neck, the softest touch. Tyler's skin woke up, and he gasped. "I want to corrupt you, Tyler," Dean whispered.

"You're seducing me?" Tyler asked. It was hard to tell

with Dean. He sort of oozed sex appeal, and Tyler didn't want to mix messages. Clarification was good.

"Yes. Is it working?"

Tyler wasn't sure about the pet name, but he loved Dean's explanation of it. "Round two?"

Dean nodded decisively, his nose tickling Tyler's neck. "Round two."

Round two happened on the pretty leather sofa, which did lead to naps in separate beds. Round three was a rough, halfhearted affair after fueling up and watching reality TV on Tyler's laptop into the evening.

By nightfall, Tyler's skin felt shocked with beard burn, his body ached from tensing so hard during his orgasms, and his brain was as calm as the eye of a storm. He sent Dean to bed upstairs with a smile and slept like the dead.

DEAN WAS SKETCHING Tyler in his brain while they lounged in the hot tub the next day. It was a red flag. A dire warning of bad things to come.

Like real feelings, feelings stronger than infatuation or lust.

He traced Tyler's lips with his eyes. They were dry from the cold weather. His hair was damp but not wet from the hot tub's steam. His neck was bitable and long and dusted with stubble.

Heavy trucks and machinery thundered down the road, working on removing the avalanche debris—a constant reminder that they weren't alone out there, that their solitude was false.

They'd been slow to start their day after yesterday's sex marathon, the sexual tension a low simmer, rather than a boiling pot. Dean was sore and out of marathon shape. He'd carb-loaded for breakfast and lunch, then suggested a dip in the hot tub to recover from the day before.

"Do you know what I hate about vacation? It's just a too-short intermission," Tyler said, leaning his head back on the edge of the hot tub. "Like a reprieve from real life, real time. Don't you think?"

Dean had been clocking time using the avalanche as the key. Post-avalanche. It was day three PA. But the arrangement with Tyler had recalibrated his entire system. There was BT and AT now. Before Tyler and After Tyler.

After Tyler had kissed him. After Tyler had come so beautifully, so spectacularly in his hand. He didn't know how he'd return to Before Tyler once the avalanche was cleared, once they returned home. He was worried he'd be using Tyler time for weeks to come.

How quickly the tables had turned.

"I do, and I don't," Dean said, carefully. Tyler was letting Dean rub his calf, steam rising around them. "It feels as if time doesn't matter because we're just stuck here waiting, but it also feels like each moment matters a whole lot."

Tyler frowned slightly like he didn't agree. Which he

probably didn't. Dean was a break for him. A rebound. A distraction from the monotony of their spoiled vacation.

Dean had learned some things about Tyler in the last three days. He'd learned that Tyler's brain did in fact run on a hamster wheel during sex, and the fun part was figuring out how to use that to their advantage. He'd learned that Tyler went nuts for rough and hard but melted into goo if you kissed the back of his neck. He'd learned that Tyler was able to spout random facts within seconds of orgasm, and that he snorted when he truly laughed.

Dean hoped that Tyler was learning things about him too, but he doubted it. Dean had too much practice hiding his true self behind a happy face. It was hard to turn that off. And honestly, Tyler seemed uninterested in looking deeper.

He saw Dean as the shallow guy he usually tried to be, and Dean didn't have anyone to blame but himself.

"Let's talk about something fun," Dean said.

"Like what?"

"First kisses."

Tyler groaned. "Can I veto?"

"If you want."

"Blah. It was a girl during Spin the Bottle in seventh grade. Not exactly life-shattering."

"Have you kissed many women?"

Tyler shook his head, his eyebrows doing that complicated thing Dean loved so much. "I had a girlfriend in high school. In retrospect, it was a mutual beard situation, but I didn't realize it at the time. She's married now. She and her wife have a kid on the way."

"Ah, we're that age. Everyone's procreating."

Tyler sat up. "What about you? First kiss?"

"A girl named Charity during Truth or Dare. I was about sixteen. Then a guy named Justice that same night, not during Truth or Dare."

"Wow. Such virtuous names."

Dean laughed. "I'd never realized."

"Two in one night. How precocious."

"Not really. I didn't hit my full potential until well into adulthood. I was a late bloomer."

Tyler smiled. "I find that hard to believe."

Dean switched to massaging Tyler's other leg.

"It's the truth."

"I bet you've been breaking hearts since middle school. Leaving weeping and gnashing of teeth in your wake."

"No." Dean stroked down Tyler's leg to his foot. "I'm friendly with my exes. Even Viggo."

"What about *your* heart?"

"Untouched so far." The only threat to Dean's heart was sitting right across from him. He wasn't sure when that had happened or when it had become so obvious to him, but Dean knew it without a doubt.

Tyler gazed out at the forest. "Should I be heartbroken about Francis? Because I'm not. I expected to be miserable for this whole vacation. I mean, I cried on the plane, but then I got here, and I'm fine."

"He sounds like a jerk."

"He was perfect for me, though. Same principles. Same goals. Career-oriented but not *too* career-oriented. Close to his family. Smart and logical. He was perfect on paper."

"Paper isn't a substitute for feelings, though. Or chemistry."

"I'm not a good judge. I can't trust my feelings."

Dean tried to decide whether it was worth putting his hypothesis about Tyler into words.

To hell with it. If Tyler got mad, he got mad.

"Maybe it's not your feelings you can't trust. Having a bulleted list of traits that makes you compatible with another man doesn't come from your heart. It comes from your head."

"You think I can't trust my head?" Tyler said suspiciously, which made sense. His brain was probably the thing Tyler trusted most in the world.

"I think you need to trust your gut every once in a while too."

"I ignored red flags," Tyler blurted.

"Like what?"

"He laughed when people got hurt, like online videos of prat falls. Once, early on, I stubbed my toe. It hurt, and reflexive tears filled my eyes. And he laughed. I must have looked funny, sort of hopping around on one foot, but that's a dick thing to do."

Dean rubbed the arch of Tyler's food and caressed every precious toe. "It is. No one should laugh at you when you're hurting."

"I hated kissing him. It wasn't terrible. It was

adequate. But no spark." Tyler swanned into Dean's space and straddled him.

"Spark should be nonnegotiable." Dean grabbed Tyler's hipbones. "Kiss me. I'll demonstrate."

Tyler bit Dean's top lip playfully, and Dean dug his fingertips into Tyler's skin.

"Careful, Tyler. Push me and I'll fuck you right out here. Show you what real chemistry feels like."

Tyler's smile was huge and bright. They touched and kissed, moving deeper into the water to stay warm. The temperature had dropped, and frost glittered in the branches of the log pole pines around them. Their breath was visible in the cold air, mixing with the steam, as their gasps got harder, as Tyler rode Dean through their swim trunks.

"You lovebirds want any jerky?"

Tyler jerked away from Dean. He about tumbled backward into the water, but Dean caught him. They both turned toward the voice that had come from the woods.

Sarg's big dog, Iceworm, barreled onto the porch and stuck his head over the side of the hot tub, lapping up some water.

"I made it myself," Sarg said as if he hadn't just interrupted a very nice makeout session. He held up a crinkled plastic baggy of jerky.

"What kind of jerky?" Tyler asked, his voice so suspicious it made Dean smile.

"Moose."

"Ah. No thanks," Tyler said.

Dean nudged him playfully. "Where's your sense of adventure?" He held out his hand. Sarg, wearing snowshoes this time instead of skis, expertly kicked them off and hopped up onto the porch. He held open the baggy, and Dean picked out a small piece.

It tasted gamier than beef jerky but wasn't bad.

"It's good," he said.

A bashful smile crossed Sarg's face. "I came to see if you needed any entertainment, but you're entertaining yourselves well enough."

Dean felt the possibility rearing up, a tiny pinch of potential between the three of them. Tyler had brought up threesomes before. Maybe this was his chance to experiment.

"You can join us," Dean said.

Sarg glanced at Tyler for permission

"Oh, uh, okay," Tyler said, flustered. "If you want. We were just talking."

Dean laughed at that, and Sarg did too. He seemed younger when he laughed. Dean suspected Sarg would look like a baby-faced boy-bander without the huge beard.

"What's so funny?" Tyler asked.

"If that's what you call *talking*, then count me in for a chat," Sarg said. He shed his coat and several layers until he was shirtless. He was large and musclebound, his chest hair surprisingly ginger. "You guys were *talking* pretty hard when I walked up."

"Oh." Tyler blushed as he seemed to remember that

he'd been grinding in Dean's lap when Sarg appeared. "*Oh, right.*"

Sarg dropped his snowpants and pulled down a pair of blue long johns, revealing teeny, neon orange briefs. His dog wiggled over and begged for some pets, which Sarg gave him, not taking his eyes off Dean and Tyler.

It was a shocking and very shockingly hot sight. An Alaskan mountain man in sexy undies petting his huge dog. It could have been in a calendar, one Dean would have paid good money for.

Tyler's jaw was on the bottom of the hot tub. Sarg let them stare, almost preening, a knowing smile on his face.

"Should I get in?" Sarg asked. "Or should we take it straight inside?"

Chapter Sixteen

"I WAS GONNA OFFER to take you snowshoeing up Salmonberry Hill, but this is less of a pain in the ass," Sarg said, water lapping at his chest. "Snow's getting mushy."

Tyler felt disoriented and excited and awkward. It was like the first time he'd been on TV, answering lightning-fast trivia questions. He didn't know what to do with his body or where to put his hands.

Dean responded to the snow comment, saying something mundane and normal to keep the conversation flowing. Tyler couldn't figure out where he should look—at Iceworm or Dean or Sarg or the steaming water.

He had to admit he was tempted by the flirtatious hints brewing between the three of them, but Dean had hammered home that communication was key when complicated sex was afoot. Tyler didn't want to step on Dean's toes or hurt Dean's feelings.

"Angel, come here."

Tyler jumped at Dean's voice, at the pet name. He splashed quickly to Dean's side and relaxed as soon as Dean threw an arm over his shoulder.

"I was just teasing. I wasn't expecting you two to jump my bones," Sarg said. "Unless you want to."

"You're into men?" Tyler said, which *duh.* He was obviously into men, but Tyler was having trouble making sense of the ricocheting thoughts in his head.

"I'm not picky. Not a lot of options out here, and I'll take what I can get. Especially if the option is as pretty as you. And fucking couples is hot."

Dean's hand tightened on Tyler's shoulder, a reminder that even the smallest hint of commitment freaked Dean out. Tyler needed to brand that on his prefrontal cortex. He needed to remember his own rules.

"We're not a couple. We're not… anything," Tyler explained. "We're only having fun." He looked toward Dean to make sure he hadn't stepped out of line.

Dean wouldn't meet his eyes but said, "For all intents and purposes, though, I'm *his* while that avalanche has us stuck here."

That was confusing for Tyler because it wasn't true, but maybe it was easier to navigate a potential threesome if Sarg saw them as a strong pair. Tyler was happy to bow to Dean's superior experience.

"Noted," Sarg said.

"So do you want to do this?" Dean asked Tyler.

Tyler felt like he was peering through a keyhole at a big, important decision. He could open the door, try something fun in a safe environment. Or he could keep it closed and wonder forever what he'd missed.

Tyler turned on the bench of the hot tub until he was facing Dean, putting his back toward Sarg. Dean touched his jaw with fingertips that were raisined from too much time in the water.

"I trust you," Tyler whispered. "Do *you* want this?"

Dean's smile was downright dirty, and Tyler's whole body tingled. "Yeah. I can make this so good for you."

Tyler nodded and opened the door to possibility, which was how, within five minutes, after cursory safety and boundary discussions, he found himself sprawled, his back to Dean's front, in the chaise lounge in his room, with Sarg's lips around his dick.

Dean was excited to see Tyler absolutely losing it as Sarg expertly sucked him off. He wanted Tyler to feel valued and treasured and sexy. It was hot seeing Sarg enjoy Tyler's body.

But Dean felt vulnerable too. He'd staked his claim. He'd made it plain as day that he was *Tyler's*. That he saw what they were doing as more than "*having fun*." And Tyler had done nothing besides blink at him.

Sarg had understood. He'd tipped his head in acknowledgment and cleared everything with both of them before jumping mouth first onto Tyler's dick.

It was a level of exposure Dean wasn't used to when he had sex, but he pushed it down and moved along. He had two beautiful men in front of him, and he didn't intend to miss it.

Tyler was the only one who was naked. Sarg was in his slutty panties, and Dean was in his swimsuit. He was thankful for the thin fabric of his trunks as Tyler squirmed in his arms, his back rubbing an intoxicating line against the whole front of Dean's body, chest to dick. Dean's legs were spread around Tyler's hips, and Tyler kept clutching at his thighs.

Tiny marks from Dean's hands and teeth marred Tyler's skin. Evidence of their time together, of the roughness and fight that turned them both on so much. They were probably invisible to Sarg, to someone who didn't know they were there, but the blemishes were spotlights to Dean.

He had been there. And *there*. And *there*.

Tyler wasn't fighting now, though. And it wasn't rough. He was luxuriating in it, in Dean's hands on his chest and Sarg taking all the time in the world to suck his cock.

"Enjoy it," Dean whispered in his ear. "Focus on how horny you're making us. Sarg—he's shaking because he loves having you in his mouth. And I could come just from feeling you against me."

Tyler turned his head toward Dean almost desperately, like he was thrashing, and Dean caught his chin. He kissed him slowly, lushly. He was trying to match the energy Sarg was bringing to the table, and Sarg apparently relished taking his time.

"Oh God, Dean," Tyler said against his mouth. "I feel like I'm being touched by an octopus."

Dean laughed softly. "In a good way?"

"Yes. So many arms. Please don't stop."

Oh, Dean would touch him forever if Tyler would let him, and that thought was *dangerous*. He lifted his hand to Tyler's throat and squeezed gently but not hard enough to cut off any air.

Tyler clawed at his arm, holding it. "I'm going to come."

Sarg moaned, urging Tyler to spill.

And Tyler, gorgeous man that he was, panted the magic word, the one that Dean had been living for since their first time. "*Harder.*"

Dean gripped his throat harder, and Tyler came, shaking and gasping for air.

Tyler turned to jelly in his arms, his head lolled back on Dean's shoulder, eyes closed. Dean looked down the long expanse of Tyler's sated body to see Sarg nuzzling the inside of Tyler's thigh.

Sarg uncurled from his kneel slowly like a sea creature rising out of the ocean. The man had seemed untamed from the start, appearing out of the wilderness, scruffy and bold.

"Come here," Dean said to Sarg. Tyler didn't stir, other than to settle his weight fully against Dean's chest.

Sarg stood and prowled toward them. His cock was straining the confines of his briefs, and Dean felt a reflexive tightening in his throat. The quick discussion ahead of time had landed on blowjobs, and fuck if Dean wasn't excited about it.

Once Sarg was within reach, Dean used his free hand—his other arm was wrapped firmly around Tyler's chest—to drag those orange undies to Sarg's knees. His cock bounced up and slapped his stomach.

Dean didn't waste any time getting the man into his mouth. He went deep fast, and Sarg cried out, threading his fingers into Dean's hair. It was overwhelming, being pinned to the chaise by Tyler's body with his mouth full of Sarg, but he didn't hate it. Dean gave into it and sucked Sarg slowly, thoroughly.

Dean nearly missed it when Tyler moved, but the loss of Tyler against his chest was hard to ignore. Tyler twisted onto his knees between Dean's legs on the chaise. Then Tyler kissed Dean's cheek, right where Sarg's cock bulged it.

Dean and Sarg both froze as Tyler worked his way from Dean's cheek to his lips stretched around Sarg's length. Dean and Tyler's lips touched, almost like a kiss. Dean moved until just the tip of Sarg's cock was in his mouth, and Tyler did kiss Dean then. Messy and full on, using his tongue to caress Sarg's crown at the same time.

"Oh, fuck me," Sarg groaned. "Fellas, that's real nice."

Tyler's hand moved down Dean's chest, finding his nipples, his belly button, and finally, the tie of his swim trunks. It was a turn-on that Tyler had never done this before. Dean was exhilarated to introduce a new world to Tyler. To give him all the pleasure possible.

In a move that belied science, Tyler bent away from Dean's mouth, from Sarg's cock, and took Dean down in one go.

Dean jolted, the sensation whole and consuming. He was not prepared for Tyler's mouth. He was never prepared for the way Tyler made him feel.

Sex with Tyler was different from what Dean was used to. Not only better but more intense too. He wasn't sure if that was due to circumstance or chemistry or *Tyler*.

But he hated that it felt special, resented it. He tried to fight it, to put distance between what was happening in his body and his… heart. To build that protective barrier that used to come to him instinctually.

But Sarg, of all people, didn't let him. Sarg grasped Dean's hair and steadily pushed deeper and deeper into his throat until Dean couldn't do anything besides focus on his breathing and react to the astonishing sensation of Tyler's lips around his cock. Dean was nothing but a circuit of exposed nerves and a scary, screaming desire to hold Tyler closer.

Dean came embarrassingly fast, Tyler's satisfied purr as he swallowed Dean's jizz echoing around them. Sarg followed him over, hitting Dean's chin and neck as Dean lost his ability to hold his own head up.

Chapter Seventeen

SARG LEFT AS QUICKLY and enigmatically as he'd appeared, giving Tyler a fleeting kiss and both of them a "Thanks, fellas" on the way out. Tyler's body felt noodly and heavy, but Dean's was all elbows and clenched muscles.

"Are you okay?" Tyler asked after too many minutes of what should have been restful silence.

Tyler had had a threesome! It hadn't sucked!

Then Sarg had left, and it wasn't awkward. There had been no uncomfortable small talk or cuddling or emotions.

Tyler was ecstatic, but Dean's tension was ruining the vibe.

"Yeah. Sorry. I'm—" Dean shook his head as he used a nearby towel, damp from them drying off after the hot tub, to wipe the stickiness off his face and neck. Tyler leaned in and kissed Dean's cheek.

Dean froze and relaxed on a shudder, so Tyler kept kissing him. His ear, his neck, the tiny scar above his lip.

"Thank you," Dean whispered as Tyler nuzzled his shoulder. The attention seemed to be helping Dean come down from the experience, so Tyler didn't see any harm in it. It wasn't breaking his rules.

Tyler's brain was telling him to throw those rules away, but he pushed the impulse away.

Ignoring the flutter of feelings after sex was a test of resolve, and Tyler liked tests. He just needed to prevent himself from falling victim to mushy endorphins. He shoved away from Dean's body and got dressed. Dean didn't move but watched him from the chaise lounge.

"That was fun," Tyler said once his favorite camp shirt was in place. It was an expensive one with pearly buttons and tiny pineapples, bananas, and pomegranates hidden among a folk-art tropical floral. The shirt felt out of place in Alaska, but it was armor for Tyler. He paired it with sweats and his warmest socks.

"I'm glad." Dean tucked his cock back in and tied his swim trunks, depriving Tyler of the free show. "Are you okay about how it went down? With Sarg leaving so quickly?"

"Yeah. I'm relieved he did. I doubt I could have acted normal with him here." A sour thought hit Tyler. He sat down heavily on his bed. "Do you wish he'd stayed? For cuddling and stuff afterward?"

Dean took way too long to answer, sending blaring alarm bells through Tyler's head. Finally, Dean said, "The only person I want to cuddle with is you. I'm very glad he left. I assume he could tell I needed… space."

"Oh." Tyler fiddled with the hem of his shirt. "Should I give you space? You're in my room, though."

Never mind that it had once been *their* room.

A slow half smile spread over Dean's face. Tyler adored that smile. He never saw Dean smile at Rosie and Leo like that. It was as if Dean saved it for him.

"I don't want space from you."

"Okay. What do you want?"

Dean languidly stood up from the chaise and advanced on Tyler. When he reached him, he fisted Tyler's hair and tipped his head back so Tyler was forced to meet his eyes. Tyler grabbed Dean's sides. He spread his fingers to touch as much of Dean's skin as possible.

"You don't want me to tell you what I want," Dean said, warning in his voice.

That warning sent mixed messages through Tyler's brain and body. It sounded sexy, but the intent caught up with Tyler before he could press for dirty talk.

Dean wasn't being flirty, and he wasn't drawing a boundary. He was abiding by *Tyler's* boundaries. He was following Tyler's rules.

What had Dean said that second morning before he'd blown Tyler's mind? That he would follow Tyler's rules until Tyler broke them himself?

There was no chance of that. Bad things happened to rule-following overthinkers when they broke the rules.

"I'm sorry," Tyler murmured. It was hard to talk with

Dean staring down at him, his expression so open and pleading. Tyler wasn't sure what he was apologizing for.

Dean let him go and took a step back. "I'm gonna shower."

Tyler wasn't ready for Dean to leave. Their conversation and Dean's vulnerability had made Tyler feel like he was wearing a too-small shirt.

"Wait… I… uh. Can we maybe… You seem off," Tyler blurted. "And when Francis was off, I assumed it was my fault. Even when it wasn't. I'd pester and pick at him until it suddenly *was* my fault, until he could come up with a complaint or a way to blame me. So I want to fix it, whatever is making you upset, now rather than later."

"Oh, angel, I'm not upset." Dean sat down beside Tyler and took his hand.

"You're acting weird. You're usually suave and *fine* after sex."

Dean laughed, and some of the discomfort loosened in Tyler's chest. "First off, I haven't been suave after sex with you at all. You're just seeing me more clearly this time."

"Or you're letting me see you more clearly."

The look Dean gave him seemed to say a million things, but Tyler didn't understand any of them. Dean's expression was wide open. "Sex with multiple partners can be intense. Sex with *you* is especially intense for *me* every time. So it's taking a second to screw my head on straight. That's not your fault, and you don't need to fix it because it's not a bad thing. It's just… a thing."

Tyler hated that answer. And loved that answer. Loved

that he wasn't the only one struggling with the intensity between them, but he hated that Dean was making it sound exceptional. It wasn't.

"Okay." Tyler nodded once, resolutely, and rose from the bed. "I think we passed the test."

"What was the test?"

"The communication-after-a-threesome test. You said that was key. So this was good… I don't know… practice."

"Right. Practice." Dean glanced around the room, almost dazed. He stood up and reached out to touch Tyler's face but dropped his hand before making contact.

Chapter Eighteen

DEAN COULDN'T SLEEP. The wind was howling outside, and when he closed his eyes, he either pictured the avalanche or Tyler's sated smile. It was a teeter-totter between a nightmare and a really great sex dream. Neither were conducive to sleep.

He tiptoed downstairs to add wood to the stove. It didn't need it. The soapstone kept the house toasty as long as they burned a fire one or two times a day, but Dean hoped the crackle of the flames would drown out the wind and his wayward thoughts.

He lay down on the couch and stared at the blaze flickering through the glass-fronted door of the stove. He was ready for this adventure to be over. There was heartache in the forecast for him. It was obvious, even if Tyler was oblivious to it.

At a certain point—Dean wasn't sure when—he'd let Tyler slip beneath his defenses. And the funny thing was

—Tyler had no idea how hard that was for Dean, how extraordinary.

Or if he did, Tyler didn't care.

Dean was raw and scraped open.

And mad. He was mad. He'd gone thirty-three years without falling for someone. He'd protected himself with a happy-go-lucky smile and a bit of a himbo attitude toward sex. He'd shielded the parts of himself that were soft. And, at the end of the day, Tyler Vlachos would be his undoing.

Absolutely ridiculous.

He found the drawing pad he'd stashed in a kitchen drawer the day before and curled up on the couch with it. He moved his woodless pencil instinctively, letting his hand shape the avalanche without really seeing the paper. When he stopped, he could tell his proportions were off, but there was anger in his lines. It was more emotional than his standard, flat drawings.

He flipped the page and started over. He could draw human form in his sleep.

Form with no image stylization at least. His specialty.

Usually, his sketches were fast and bare bones, but he took his time, considering every line, every fluid lift of his pencil. He wished he were using compressed charcoal, but it was upstairs in his bag.

"That's me," Tyler said from the doorway to his room, and Dean jumped. His pencil slipped and made a dark, jagged line down the page. He hadn't heard the door open. "I'm sorry. I didn't mean to scare you. But that's me." Tyler was sleep-rumpled and so hot it burned Dean to look at him.

He blinked down at his pad. He couldn't deny it. The wavy hair, the bare chest, the bunched-up shirt he'd yet to give a pattern, the birthmark on the knee. "I told you I was going to draw your O face."

Tyler laughed his sweet, surprised laugh and sat down next to Dean. Tyler examined the drawing. All the inadequacies of Dean's life piled up in his throat.

"This is good," Tyler said.

"It's decent. I mean, you're beautiful." Dean analyzed his work, already seeing mistakes and things he'd have to fix. "But this"—he tapped the paper—"pales in comparison to reality. I like your glasses, by the way."

Tyler blushed. "I look attractive here, though. It's weird that you see me that way."

"As sexy?"

"No. As a model. Someone worth drawing."

"A muse." Dean smiled as Tyler's blush deepened. "Want a quick lesson? I'll teach you." He held up his pencil.

Tyler shook his head. He kept glancing at the drawing pad. "No, I want you to teach me something else."

"What's that?" Dean asked, but he already knew. Tyler's body was changing in front of Dean's eyes, a growing erection tenting Tyler's sweatpants.

"Come to bed with me," Tyler whispered almost like it was a secret.

Dean closed the drawing pad and set his pencil aside. "Of course."

"Bring the toys?"

Dean stood slowly, putting himself in Tyler's personal space. He dipped his head to Tyler's ear. "You let me in your bed, and I'm going to wreck it. I'm going to take you apart until you're begging me."

"Begging you for what?" Tyler asked, his voice defiant.

To stay.

Dean licked Tyler's neck.

To stay. He wanted Tyler to beg him to stay, but Dean would never, ever say that.

DEAN WAS MOVING SLOWER than Tyler could handle. When he'd found Dean in the living room, when he'd seen himself through Dean's eyes, Tyler had longed to rip Dean's clothes off and crawl all over him.

It was like seeing a slice of Dean's soul. That picture was different from the sketches of random body parts he'd seen Dean make days before. The drawing of Tyler had *feeling*. It portrayed Tyler as hotter and better in a million ways than he was in real life, and it had been too much.

He'd needed to direct them back to calmer waters, to their temporary break from reality. To their sex arrangement with zero emotions and zero friendship and zero future.

It felt safer in bed than wherever Dean's art was going to lead them.

"You have to choose a safeword," Dean said as he slipped a piece of fabric down Tyler's arm. They were half-undressed, and Dean kept pumping the brakes on Tyler's speed and lust. "If you want this silk around your wrists, and I know you do, you have to have a safeword."

"That's not silk," Tyler griped. "It's satin."

Dean smiled and pinned Tyler's wrists above his head near the metal headboard. "What's the difference?"

"Silk is a natural fiber fabric made from silkworms. Satin is a weave used to make fabric look shiny."

"Keep going." Dean moved against Tyler, pressing his still-covered cock against Tyler's side. "Your nerdy brain turns me on."

"This is satin polyester. It's cheaper than silk, nonbiodegradable, and—" Tyler lost his train of thought as Dean straddled his waist and looped the fabric through a slat on the headboard.

"Go on."

"Silk can be a satin weave, though."

"Angel, you need a safeword right now."

"*Stop*?"

"No. What if you say, '*Stop* teasing me. *Stop* torturing me. *Stop*, I'm about to come,' but what you really want is for me to keep going?"

Tyler groaned. "Promises, promises."

"The word has to be weird and easy for you to conjure out of nowhere."

Tyler stared up at Dean above him. He was so gorgeous, and his consideration plucked at a deep part of

Tyler's emotional control. "I don't know. Captain Crunch?"

Dean smiled. "Cool. Cereal. Mine's *red*."

"Red! You said it had to be weird."

Dean just laughed and kissed Tyler's cheek. He finally tied each end of the fabric around Tyler's wrists and stripped off the rest of their clothes.

They'd played around with restraint, but it was always at Tyler's mercy—Dean commanding Tyler to hold on to the arm of the sofa and not let go, Dean halfheartedly pinning Tyler's wrists down.

Using an actual restraint that Tyler couldn't easily game was exhilarating.

"I'd learn rope play for you," Dean said, kissing the pad of Tyler's thumb. Before Tyler could react to that strange admission, Dean tugged on the fabric. "Is this too tight?"

Tyler shook his head. "It's perfect."

Dean hummed and started his descent down Tyler's body, giving whispery kisses to every ticklish part he could find. Tyler thrashed because he loved trying to writhe away and not be able to.

"Harder, Dean." The softness of Dean's mouth was making Tyler's skin tingle. When Dean reached Tyler's inner thigh, he bit down sharply. Tyler gasped, "Yes," and let his legs fall open.

"You're gorgeous like this," Dean murmured. "At my mercy."

"I'm not at your—oh fuck."

Dean pressed slick fingers inside Tyler roughly, curling

them hard. Tyler bucked. He was oversensitive, his body not quite ready to relax into the floaty sensations, which only made it better.

For all Tyler's complaints about Dean's tortoise impression earlier, Dean was moving fast now. He replaced his fingers with a curved glass wand. It was cold and harder than flesh or even Tyler's long-forgotten silicone dildo.

Tyler's foot shot straight out in surprise. He gave a little whimper of shock. Dean caught his ankle and kissed it gently, so at odds with the rough way he was fucking him.

"That's it. I love the struggle, angel."

"I hate that name," Tyler lied.

Dean grinned and tipped the wand firmly against Tyler's prostate. Tyler's mouth dropped open, but no sound came out. He tried to move his hands to instinctively push Dean away and met resistance.

Tyler felt both frozen and turned on, torn between the too-much sensation in his ass and the too-good feeling of being tied up.

"Can you come hands-free?" Dean asked.

"What? Of course not." Tyler knew it was possible for some people but that was surely, like, a total unicorn anomaly.

"Good."

"Why is that good?"

Dean pulled the wand out and set it aside. Within seconds, he'd expertly rolled a condom down his length and drove inside Tyler.

Tyler's body fought it, but he craved the rough treatment, the frantic look in Dean's eyes. He loved that Dean was so hot and bothered that he couldn't even slow down to baby Tyler through the first thrusts.

"It's good because I don't want you to shoot without warning. Now"—Dean planted his fists beside Tyler's restrained arms—"I'm gonna wreck you."

Tyler didn't doubt it. They'd fooled around plenty, but it was the first time Dean had been inside him in that particular way. He was having trouble getting leverage to move with Dean, to fuck back, and he realized that was the point.

"That's it," Dean said sweetly in his ear. "You can't move. You're mine, so just take it, Ty."

He slowly adjusted to Dean's length and rhythm. Dean surrounded him. His body was over Tyler's, his lips on Tyler's skin, his face the only thing in Tyler's field of vision.

"It should be illegal for you to wear those glasses," Dean muttered, riding him hard. "If I was lucky enough to see you in those every day, I'd never stop touching you."

Tyler tilted his head back on a gasp. His thighs clenched, and a ceaseless tremble moved through his whole being like it was on a loop controlled by Dean's magic cock.

"I want… I want to…" Tyler couldn't force the words out. His brain wasn't working. His vision was hazy.

"Want to?"

"Banter with you, but it feels too—" Tyler shook his head.

"I hope you planned to finish that sentence with *fabulous*."

"Uh huh. Yeah. I think I lied about coming hands-free." It was the fabric around his wrists. It had to be. It was fucking up his head, sending extra signals to his cock and nuts.

"Can't have that." Dean gave him an evil smile, kissed him quickly on the lips, and pulled out.

Chapter Nineteen

TYLER WAS DRIPPING WITH SWEAT. Time had no meaning. He felt half-delirious.

Dean licked a line up the center of Tyler's chest and pushed a new toy inside him. Tyler didn't try to see what it was. They were on their third or fourth cycle at that point.

Dean would fuck him until Tyler was at his breaking point. Then he would pull out and use a toy. Rinse. Repeat.

The toy was always different enough from Dean's cock, which was *substantial* and *curved* and frankly the *best* ever, to feel like a reprieve.

This toy was small and slipped inside easily.

"Your wrists okay?" Dean asked.

The satin fabric wasn't tied tight, and Tyler's arms were resting slack against the bed. "Yeah."

"You can feel your fingers?"

"Uh-huh."

Tyler started to lift his head to get a better look at Dean, but then the toy jumped to life in his body.

He yelped, and his hips and back arched off the bed. Everything else Dean had used on him had been low-tech. Nothing with vibration. Nothing that required a battery or remote or app.

The prostate massager hit him with a concentrated, pulsing buzz. He twisted his head back and forth. He yanked his arms, moaning when they barely moved and the fabric pulled at his skin.

"Good or bad, Tyler?" Dean asked. His voice was hoarse, and his hair was sweaty too. Tyler wasn't the only one who was wrecked.

"Kinda both."

It took a beat for Tyler to realize Dean was putting a condom and lube on *him*. It was the first time Dean had touched his cock, and Tyler cried out.

Unexpectedly, the vibrations decreased, probably from the remote in Dean's palm, and Tyler could breathe without his lungs seizing.

Dean straddled his waist. Tyler saw what was about to happen, but he couldn't quite comprehend it. Dean lowered himself down onto Tyler's cock. The silky slip of Dean's body, the pressure and heat, the vibration inside him.

"Stop. I'm… I can't stop it," Tyler gasped.

He'd managed not to beg for a much-needed release—a slight point of pride—but now that it was about to happen, he didn't want it to. He didn't want this to end.

"Fight it," Dean said. His expression was fierce, color high on his cheeks and down his sweaty chest. "You're incredible. So hard and so fucking right, Tyler Vlachos. So fight it."

"Last-naming me is not helping." Tyler squeezed his eyes shut. "Please, Dean."

Dean moved faster, a deliberate slide up and down his cock. Tyler wanted to grab Dean. To stop him or hold him closer. To claw at his back and fist his hair and press fresh bruises into his thick, glorious thighs. But he couldn't. He was immobilized, not only by the strip of fabric tying his wrists to the bed but also by the pleasure shooting from head to toe.

"Dean. Oh no." Tyler's fingers clenched around the satin tie.

"You can fight it." Dean slipped his fingers into Tyler's hair and licked across Tyler's bottom lip. Tyler lifted his chin to kiss Dean more fully, hoping it would distract from the crash of orgasm that Tyler was struggling against.

But it didn't distract him. It detonated him.

Dean held him through the shaking. Through the overwhelmed tear that leaked from the corner of his left eye and the dizzying rush of sensation that fried his last brain cells as completely as it did every nerve ending in his body.

Dean's caveman brain was shouting, *Mine, mine, mine*, even as his logical side was telling him to slow down. To stop pushing. To be a good guy.

Dean didn't want to be good. Going hard and fast and rough felt like exactly what Tyler needed and wanted and deserved.

He pulled off Tyler's cock, took care of the full condom as quickly as he could, and yanked the knots loose from Tyler's wrists.

With his hands free, Tyler immediately snatched at Dean's hair, grabbing onto it and tugging hard. "Inside me. Get inside me," Tyler demanded.

Yeah, that man didn't want Dean to be a good guy either.

Dean removed the toy from Tyler's ass and claimed it for his own. Tyler twitched but didn't shove Dean away; he clutched Dean closer. Dean moved at the exact tempo to get himself off quickly, to use Tyler the way Tyler was begging with his hands and his lips to be used.

The perfect man. Perfect not just in bed, not just because Dean had never had sex so intense. Tyler had a perfect mind. Perfect and lovely and right.

Dean kissed Tyler hard, taking his lips and branding them with his own. Tyler held Dean's hair with one fist and scratched a sharp line down Dean's back with the other hand.

It amped Dean up and shocked him, that prickle of pain mixed with pleasure. He reached back, grabbed Tyler's arm, and pinned it to the side of Tyler's head.

Dean was so close he was trembling. He expected

Tyler to fight his hold, especially after being restrained for so long. But Tyler didn't. He curled his fingers into Dean's and held his hand.

And Dean lost it. His mind. His heart. Control. He lost everything.

Chapter Twenty

THE SUN HADN'T RISEN YET, but Tyler was wide awake. He'd slept for a few hours during the night but had woken up hot and sweaty in Dean's arms. Dean hadn't stirred since he'd closed his eyes, almost like he hadn't slept well all week. And maybe he hadn't. Tyler didn't know because they hadn't shared a bed.

Not once.

It had been one of Tyler's rules until Dean's plaintive eyes and drugging kisses had undone Tyler's resolve.

He hadn't even thought about kicking Dean out.

It was bad, bad, bad.

He wiggled out from under the covers and looked back at Dean. He had a hand outstretched toward where Tyler had been sleeping.

"Fuck," Tyler mouthed. He gathered up clothes and tiptoed to the door. He was out of practice, but he managed to sneak out of the room without Dean waking up.

The kitchen wasn't far enough away from the disaster in his bed, so he bundled up and went outside. Since the outdoors kept trying to kill him, Tyler didn't go farther than the lake. The world was cast in a flat light blue like a weird photo filter.

The edges of the lake had refrozen into a thin film. He tapped the toe of his boot against it, and it crumpled, melting into nothing.

The center of the lake was solid, though. The beacon flashed in the dim light, signaling that spring breakup was not yet complete.

Tyler stood there in the cold for a long time, mind running on overdrive.

Vacation wasn't real. The avalanche, the separation from their friends, the wild sex. It was like a movie. The good bits weren't going to follow him home.

The crunch of boots sounded behind him, and his heart leapt to his throat in excitement. It was quickly followed by a cascade of dread and panic and distrust. His emotions were all over the place, and he wasn't sure which one to grasp onto.

"I brought you coffee," Dean said, his voice low and careful.

"Thanks." Tyler took the steaming mug and sipped it. Dean had made it with just enough creamer to wake up Tyler's sweet tooth. He tried not to dwell on that. It meant nothing that Dean paid attention to how Tyler liked his coffee.

"Those mountains are turning pink, but the sun's not up yet," Dean said. He had his own coffee. Black with a pinch of sugar. Tyler knew how Dean liked his as well.

The peaks across the lake were brightening quickly, going from blush to hot pink before their eyes.

"It's beautiful," he murmured. "That phenomenon has a name. Alpine-something? Alpen-something?" Tyler shook his head, frustrated that he didn't know. "I'll research it later."

Dean took Tyler's coffee and placed it on the wooden bench by their feet. Tyler let Dean wrap him in his arms and rest his chin on Tyler's shoulder.

"Watch with me," he said in Tyler's ear.

Tyler nodded. They watched in silence as the sun made an appearance. As it got lighter and lighter outside, Tyler's tension ratcheted up. Anxiety, sharp and metallic, sliced through him. Dean turned him so they were facing each other.

Dean's expression seemed to say *Are you okay?* and *What's wrong?* and *It's going to be fine* all at once. But he didn't say any of those things out loud.

Instead, he cradled Tyler's cold cheeks in his hands.

Their mouths met—the most natural thing in the world.

Tyler sighed and slipped his hands underneath Dean's jacket and shirt. His skin was warm and smooth. Dean tugged him closer. They kissed slowly, almost tentatively. Shyly, like a first kiss.

It was the best kiss Tyler had ever had.

He pushed against Dean chest. Pushed until they

separated, and that separation carved out a piece of Tyler's soul. It hurt.

"What was that?" Tyler asked.

"What did it feel like?" Dean said, cheeky humor in his voice, but it came out wrong.

"Dean." Tyler frowned. He needed to get control of himself.

He needed *Dean* to get control of himself.

"It's beautiful out here, and I wanted to kiss you. You deserve kisses like that, Tyler. Kisses in epic places. Kisses that are romantic and good and *meaningful*."

"It's not sex." Tyler took two steps away before rounding back on him. "We said sex only, and unless you're about to drop to your knees and blow me in this godawful slush, that wasn't sex."

Dean lifted his hands in a so-what gesture. "I broke your rules. You're right. And I'm sorry." Dean placed his hand against Tyler's chest. Against his heart.

Tyler shook his head, denying all the things Dean wasn't saying. "You don't care when things end, remember?" Tyler said, rattling off the reasons a relationship would never work with Dean. "You said 'fuck feelings' and 'fuck relationships.' You don't open up to people or let your partners in."

"I've never been more honest. I've told you in a million ways what I feel for you, Tyler. And I've tried to do it while following your awful rules."

"No." Tyler slipped in a patch of mud in his haste to put space between them but managed to stay on his feet.

“These fucking boots.” He kicked a rock toward the lake, and it skittered down the bank. “This was a rebound.”

“A rebound of what?” Dean advanced on him. “A partner who didn’t appreciate that you’re smart and weird and wonderful? Who broke your trust six ways to Sunday and never made you feel the way I make you feel? A guy who broke up with me and all I felt was relief? They were stopgaps in our lives.”

“No, this is the vacation. The stopgap.”

“Not for me. Not for me at all.” Dean clutched Tyler’s shoulders. “Trust yourself, Tyler. Be honest with yourself. Because I know you feel this big, scary thing too. This is real between us.”

The sound of a vehicle coming from the direction of the avalanche stopped the ugly words from spilling out of Tyler’s mouth.

“Later. We’ll finish this later,” Tyler said.

He *was* being honest with himself.

Wasn’t he?

He’d been told in therapy once that overthinking was a defense mechanism. That it disconnected him from his intuition and made it hard to recognize and trust his feelings.

He planned and overplanned for every possible situation until he was more to-do list than real-life instinct.

With Francis, he had logic-ed his way into a relationship that was perfect on paper, only to be completely fucking screwed because he didn’t trust his intuition when it told him that perfect on paper wasn’t good enough.

But his emotions weren't safe right then. And yeah, he didn't trust them.

He sure as hell didn't trust Dean's either.

The large truck slowed down. Dean gave the driver a tight smile, and they both lifted their hands in a friendly gesture that had obviously been drilled into their Midwestern heads.

"Dean," Tyler hissed through his teeth. "Where did that truck come from?"

He had a sinking feeling it was from Silverbrite Springs. Which meant—

The passenger side window rolled down, and their fantasy bubble cracked and crashed apart. Wrangell leaned over from the driver's seat and smiled.

"Well, aren't you two a sight for sore eyes. I'm Wrangell, by the way. You must be Davey," Wrangell said, introducing himself to Dean.

"Nice to meet you," Dean said. He sounded dazed and didn't correct Wrangell about his name. "The avalanche debris is cleared, I guess?"

"Yep! You'll see machinery coming through this morning. Hopefully, everyone can move freely by late morning, early afternoon. Some fancy scientific forecasters are going to do an evaluation to determine there's no risk of another slush flow. I'm on my way to pick them up. They broke down up the road."

Wrangell continued on about avalanche forecasters and snow rangers, spouting the kind of information that Tyler normally would have eaten up, but his head was too full. All he heard was gibberish.

"Sorry," Wrangell patted his steering wheel. "I've been staying at Sarg's place in the hills, and it's lonely as hell. I'm talking your ear off, and it's too early in the morning for that."

"Sarg's home is on the Silverbrite Springs side of the avalanche?" Tyler asked.

"Yeah. Did you meet my elusive brother?"

"We met him," Dean said, dark humor in his voice.

"Where has he been staying then?" Tyler asked. They hadn't seen him going in or out of Brooks's cabin. He always appeared from the woods.

"Your guess is as good as mine," Wrangell said. "I try not to worry about it. Anyway, Brooks is driving your friends back later today. I'm sorry your spring break was such a bust."

"It was okay," Tyler said, but the words tasted sour.

Wrangell said his goodbyes and took off down the gravel road. Other vehicles followed like he'd said they would.

"We better go clean up," Tyler said. He wanted to confirm there was no evidence of their little arrangement lying around.

Dean made a clicking noise with his tongue that plainly communicated his disappointment.

There was something about *disappointment* that completely shredded Tyler. Maybe it was a relic of being an overachieving gay kid growing up. Maybe it was because he worked in education, and there was nothing worse than disappointing his boss or his students or his students' parents.

Whatever it was, disappointment fucked him up. He opened his mouth to apologize, but Dean didn't let him.

Dean shook his head once, hard, and said, "Let's go, angel. I've got to put away my dirty drawings of you."

Chapter Twenty-One

THE TENSION in the cabin had been suffocating Tyler for three hours.

And Dean—*fuck that guy*.

Dean joked with Tyler. He didn't avoid him. He kept up lighthearted banter that Tyler had no hopes of reciprocating.

Basically, Dean was acting like nothing was wrong when *everything* was wrong.

Everything was different.

It was so typical. Another mind game like their first almost-kiss in the sauna. The purpose was to wind Tyler up, to make him feel off-kilter. Dean wanted the upper hand, which was ridiculous because Tyler had been giving him much, much more than the upper hand for four freaking days!

What if Dean's admission, his pretty speech down at Skipper Lake, all those broken rules, had been a mind game too?

What if Dean was already regretting it? What if Tyler had only been an available body because Rosie and Leo were stuck on the other side of the avalanche?

God, there was no way that was true. Was there?

"You okay?" Dean asked after Tyler tried several times, and failed, to open the dishwasher.

"Yeah. Just..." *Freaking out*. "Just thinking."

Overthinking.

"Want to share with the class?"

"No." Tyler glared at Dean. He was so furious with him. Disproportionately furious. "Do you?"

"I'm not the one thinking so hard I can't use a kitchen appliance."

"Are you going to tell Rosie and Leo?"

"Tell them what?" Dean sat down languidly at the kitchen table, his stupidly long legs stretched out.

"About"—Tyler waved his hands—"everything! Why are you acting so weird?"

"Tyler, I say this with all the kindness in my heart, but I'm not the one acting weird. Do you want me to keep our secret affair secret?"

"I don't know. I don't know how this usually works with you, Dean," Tyler snapped. "You're the one who does stuff like this all the time."

"Might I remind you I was also in a year-long relationship until two weeks ago," Dean said placidly. "I do not do stuff like this all the time."

"Yeah, and you've spent the whole trip trying to convince anyone who will listen that that relationship was a big ol' nothing burger."

Dean stood up. He was so tall, but it was the first time he'd used his height to make a point. "It *was* nothing. Why are you so bothered?"

"I'm not bothered." Tyler finally got the dishwasher open, only to realize the dishes inside hadn't been washed. He slammed it shut and jabbed the start button. He was too angry to turn around.

"Tyler," Dean said, his voice too gentle.

"No. Stop. Whatever you're about to say in *that voice*, I don't want to hear it."

"Why not?"

"Because it hurts, okay. I hate feeling like this, and—"

The cabin door creaking open stopped Tyler in his tracks. Playtime was over. Fight time was over.

Rosie and Leo rushed in, happy and light and giggly. A sunbeam to the thunder of Tyler's emotions.

Leo was talking a thousand miles a minute about their adventures. He'd given Tyler two hugs in his excitement.

Once the hellos were out of the way, Leo plopped down at the table. "So what did you two get up to while we were gone?"

Dean sat down too. He was relaxed and smiling and manspreading all over the place. "Went on a few walks. Saw a moose. Watched a show called *Bermuda Triangle of Love* and some of one called *Throuple Threat* about Broadway actors in a polycule. Met the other Rossi triplet. Enjoyed the hot tub. Tyler read a book. Honestly, it was nice and boring. Just what I needed."

A strange, silent beat passed between Dean and Leo.

Tyler suspected they had a whole, nonverbal conversation that he had no hopes of understanding.

"What's wrong with you?" Leo asked Dean. "Are you all right?"

Dean's gaze flicked so quickly toward Tyler that he almost thought he'd imagined it.

"I'm fine." Dean laughed, and it sounded real, but Tyler knew with every fiber of his being that it wasn't.

Leo frowned and leaned toward Dean. "Hey, let's go upstairs to chat."

Rosie observed the exchange, her mouth tight.

"I said I'm fine." Dean cocked his head playfully, but anger—crystal-clear anger—flashed through his eyes, there and gone again in a flash.

An avalanche of realizations crashed through Tyler at once.

It was a mask, not a mind game. Dean's mask was so practiced and so firmly in place that Tyler had missed it.

But Dean's best friends hadn't. Leo and Rosie had seen it immediately.

They could tell Dean's veneer of nonchalance meant something was very, very wrong. That Dean was in pain.

Dean had all but asked Tyler to go steady on the shore of the lake, and Tyler had panicked and left Dean hanging because there no way Dean actually cared about him. No way it was anything but a sex-fueled holiday.

But the difference between Dean with his walls up versus down was stark.

Dean's walls had been down for days, Tyler realized.

The late-night drawing of Tyler.

The way Dean looked at him like Tyler was leveling him just by being himself.

The sweet words and promises during sex that seemed to be about intimacy and connection and the future.

Dean claiming to be *Tyler's* while in the hot tub with Sarg.

Oh God.

Tyler's overactive mind provided him with moment after moment after moment where Dean had shown Tyler exactly who he was and exactly how good they could be together. How real they could be. He'd shown Tyler his authentic self.

He'd shown Tyler how much he cared.

Tyler hadn't seen it until he was presented with how skilled Dean was at being fake. At pretending not to care about anything at all.

"You've got your insouciance dialed up to a ten, my friend," Leo said lightly, handling Dean with kid gloves. "Let's go for a walk."

Dean was trying to protect himself from Tyler because Tyler was hurting him.

It was unbearable to Tyler. Intolerable.

"I'm going to fall for you," Tyler blurted. He wasn't even facing Dean when he said it. He was looking at Rosie, who froze with her hand halfway to her face. "If we keep seeing each other when we go home, I'm going to fall for you."

He risked a glance at Dean, whose eyes were saucers.

"What's happening?" Leo whispered.

"So, you know, it's not going to be a nothing burger

on my end, and that's scary," Tyler finished. It was the most anticlimactic confession ever, but he was trusting his gut for once in his life. Acting before thinking himself into a hole.

No one moved.

"Yep. So I'll keep talking if I have to," Tyler said, nervousness bubbling up inside and making him lose control of his mouth. "I never want to hurt you, Dean, and I can see now that you are. I'm so sorry. You're amazing. And not just because you're hot and mind-blowing in bed." He saw Rosie cover her mouth with her hand, probably in secondhand embarrassment for him. She had an engagement ring on her ring finger. "Wow. You're engaged. Congrats." He turned back to Dean. "I should have told you that at the lake. That you're more than I deserve. You're more than anyone deserves. The real you is pretty fucking great. You're not shallow. You're an incredibly talented artist. You're not all the jokey, horrible things you say about yourself. I'm scared that I'm not good enough, and that you'll see that so freaking quick. And that's terrifying."

Shocked silence echoed through the cabin. Tyler wanted to sink through the floor and never see any of them ever again.

Except Dean. He wanted to see Dean every day.

He opened his mouth to keep going. *He would.* He would tell Dean that he loved the way Dean had kissed him during the sunrise. That he thought Dean was brilliant and that teaching was a remarkable, generous use of his talent. It made him shine brighter.

But Dean stood up before Tyler managed to continue word-vomiting all over the room. Dean slowly walked around the table.

He stopped and kissed the top of Leo's head. "Congratulations." His eyes didn't leave Tyler.

When Dean made it to Rosie's perch on the back of the couch, he pressed his lips quickly to her cheek. "Congratulations."

By the time Dean made it to him, Tyler's breath was coming in bursts, and he felt overexposed and burnt by the attention.

Dean grabbed his cheeks, held them, and stared down at Tyler.

No walls. Just fierceness and affection.

"I want you. I want to watch TV with you and drag down your trivia team at the bar. I want the tough conversations. I want the friendship. I want to sleep next to you every night. I've wanted that since the first night here in Alaska, when next to you I felt peace for the first time in so fucking long."

"First night?" Tyler said. He hadn't realized. His whole world tried to recalibrate with all the new information hitting him at once.

"Yeah, angel. First night. You're beautiful. You're funny and smart and so maddening. And I want this to mean something."

Tyler clutched at Dean's shirt. "It does. It does."

"I am so irritated with you," Dean said, his voice gruff and full of tenderness.

Tyler's face split into a smile he couldn't control. "Irritation is better than nothing."

"I feel *everything*. I feel so much." He pressed Tyler's hand against the drumbeat of his heart. "For you."

"I think Francis stealing my money was the best thing to ever happen to me."

Dean laughed, and Tyler saw infinite emotion in Dean's eyes—the exhilaration, the astonishment, the relief. Nothing was hidden.

"I think a moose almost killing me was the best thing to ever happen to me," Dean said.

"Yeah." Tyler nodded, uncontrollably happy. He was about to cry, and he'd never cried out of joy. "Yeah. That was great. Top five moment for sure." He yanked Dean closer. "Come here."

Tyler kissed Dean. A reckless crash of lips that softened and sweetened. It felt incredible to break his last rule. To have broken all of them, one by one. The last threads of Tyler's fear melted away like ice under the summer sun.

Tyler deepened the kiss, let his mind rush with possibility and his body sing at the rightness of having Dean in his arms.

Dean held onto Tyler like he was the most precious person in the whole world, like he was never letting Tyler go, and Tyler believed it.

Epilogue

FIFTEEN MONTHS LATER

"ALASKA HAS the highest number of plane crashes per capita in the world," Tyler said.

Dean glanced up from the boutonniere he was trying to pin on himself and gaped at the love of his life.

"Tyler, why would you tell me that an hour before we get on a plane?"

Tyler was sprawled back on the chaise lounge—one that brought back lots of good memories. He was already dressed for the wedding, wearing navy chinos and a crisp white-and-blue floral camp shirt. He'd made an attempt at taming his chin-length hair, but the hair was winning that fight. Dean wanted to eat him alive.

"I'm just saying... Out of all the people in the world, we're trusting Sargent Rossi to land us on a glacier safely?" Tyler said, his voice full of humor that Dean suddenly didn't share. "I'd rather not know what my pilot's underwear looks like. I'd prefer my pilot be a total mystery. Makes it easier to believe they're competent."

"You weren't worried about Sarg's competence last night," Dean said. Tyler shot Dean a naughty smile. They'd utilized the Chum Smoke Cabins' sauna in the middle of the night, and Sarg had been a fun addition to the sweaty experience. "He takes tourists out there several times a week. We'll be fine." Dean was mainly reassuring himself at that point. He planted his hands on both sides of Tyler's head, caging him in. "You're trying to rile me up."

Tyler grinned. He was relaxed, his body loose and pliant after several days of banging as much as possible in the very cabin where it had all begun.

It had been over a year, and Dean had never felt safer or happier. Tyler saw and understood Dean in a way that both settled and sparked him.

"Is it working?" Tyler asked.

"Angel, we only have an hour before we're supposed to meet the wedding party at the airstrip."

"I know for a fact you can tie me up, light me up, and wring me out in less than an hour. I'd probably have time to shower again."

Dean shook his head at the firecracker of a man below him. He remembered when Tyler could hardly hint at sex without blushing. What had happened to his shy prude of a boyfriend?

"I have to finish my best man speech," Dean said reluctantly. He would have loved to take Tyler apart.

"Your speech that's not a speech."

"Yes." Dean sat down on the edge of their bed. The sun-streaked woods beyond their open window had soft forest floors covered in pine needles, mushrooms growing from every stump, and creeks galore. It was a fairy world as beautiful in the summer as the snow-capped spring.

"Stop fiddling with it. They're going to adore it," Tyler said.

Dean wasn't sure he agreed.

Tyler stood and picked up the boutonniere Dean had abandoned. He pinned it to Dean's chest before cupping Dean's chin. "Your art is worthy of this moment, sweetheart."

Dean tried to stare down at his lap. Tyler didn't let him, using a firm hand to keep Dean's head tilted up. Tyler didn't call Dean *sweetheart* very often, but it completely shattered Dean when he did. And to use it then, in a reference to Dean's art and insecurities—oh damn.

Tyler smiled and lightly brushed Dean's lips with his thumb. "Do you know how much I love you?" Tyler asked like it was a real question and not a rhetorical one.

"I hope it's even half as much as I love you. Because that's a whole hell of a lot."

"We come here to Alaska, and everything is so huge and vast and wild. There's a forest that goes on forever and mountains that rise straight out of the ocean. Last time, it was snow and ice that seemed endless and terrifying. It leaves me speechless and overwhelmed and awestruck. And that wonder doesn't touch the depth of feeling I have for you."

Dean laughed and tried to rub the rush of emotion out of his eyes. "Damn it, Tyler. What the hell?"

A huge, unburdened smile split Tyler's face. "I'm not sorry. They're going to love your speech. They're going to think it's amazing." He smacked a kiss against Dean's lips. "Now put on your hiking boots, and let's go."

THERE WERE eight people attending Rosie and Leo's wedding on Skipper Glacier—Rosie's sister, Sasha, and her husband, Perry; Rosie's brother, Benji, and his partner, William; Leo's parents; and Dean and Tyler.

It was an unusual wedding but no less full of devotion for that fact. Rosie had told Tyler she'd never planned to get married again, but they wanted to get Leo on her health insurance, which seemed like as loving and modern a reason as any Tyler could think of. She had been the one to propose, a detail Tyler and Dean had missed amidst their own drama. Not much else in Rosie and Leo's life was changing. Not her last name, their finances, their living arrangements, or their hard-fought independence. Tyler was proud of Rosie and Leo for continuing to pave their own paths, together and apart. A piece of paper wasn't going to change that.

The flight, which only took thirty minutes from the airstrip outside Silverbrite Springs, didn't actually scare Tyler. He trusted Sarg. It was a bluebird day with no wind, and Dean held his hand the whole time.

They all fit on Sarg's twelve-seater plane. The photographer—whom Rosie had found via a referral from Brooks—sat next to Sarg in the copilot's seat.

As they flew over Skipper Lake, Sarg said through the headsets they were wearing, "There's the scar from your avalanche on our left."

Tyler and Dean peered out the window. They had driven and walked past the avalanche location several times since arriving a few days before, and fragments of leftover damage were visible from the road. But from the air, it was as if someone had scraped off a whole swath of mountain. There were no trees growing in that area, and the ground was lighter than the surrounding mountain.

"He called it our avalanche," Dean said in Tyler's ear.

"We shouldn't be proud of that."

They cruised through the mountains, Sarg pointing out hidden waterfalls and wildlife before making a landing on the icefield near Skipper Glacier.

From there, they walked about a hundred yards onto the glacier, giving the wedding a jaw-dropping backdrop of neon-blue cracks and crevasses.

It was strange to be on a huge swath of ice in the middle of July. It was colder on the glacier than down in Silverbrite Springs, but the sun warmed their skin.

Dean was Leo's best man, but Leo was an incredibly lowkey groom. The whole wedding was lowkey. A beautiful location in the Alaskan summer sun, wildflower boutonnieres and bouquets, a champagne toast, and lunch afterward at Dog Salmon Saloon. No one was even wearing a suit, and Rosie's short pink dress was from a vintage clothing store. The most difficult aspect of the wedding had been finding boots that looked okay with his outfit but would hopefully prevent any slipping.

Without fanfare, the ceremony started. Rosie and Leo faced each other with Benji officiating between them. Everyone else stood in a semicircle and watched.

Leo and Rosie promised themselves to each other in such a simple, heartfelt way it almost brought tears to Tyler's eyes.

It did bring tears to Leo's. Tyler hadn't pegged him for a weeper, but Leo laughed and sniffled through the whole ceremony. Rosie smiled and held his hands, steady as a rock.

After they exchanged rings and were pronounced married, Leo gently framed Rosie's throat with his hands and kissed her. SAs Leo pulled away, she lightly patted his cheek and bit his bottom lip. It was sweet and also undeniably sexy.

With the ceremony over, Rosie did the honors of popping the champagne and giving everyone generous pours. Sasha gave her speech first as matron-of-honor. It was funny and brash and short.

Then it was Dean's turn. Tyler leaned in and kissed his cheek. "You've got this."

Dean nodded. He held up his champagne flute before seeming to realize it would be hard to show the book of drawings and hold the glass at the same time. Tyler rushed in and grabbed the flute. He would always be there to back up his man.

"Once I started writing this speech to celebrate my two best friends, I realized that the words wouldn't come, but inspiration did. Those of you who know me know I don't share original art very often. But as I thought of the things that bind Rosie and Leo together, the things that make them so wonderful for each other, I couldn't get the words on the page... just the pictures."

He opened to the first page in the book and showed the crowd. It was a drawing of Rosie and Leo from behind. They were curled up together on a bench, her head on his shoulder, fireworks in the distance. Tyler knew, from Dean's explanation, that it was from a Fourth of July sex party, but there was nothing explicit. It only showed their pure tenderness for each other.

"Rosie and Leo take care of each other. They are in each other's corner one hundred percent," Dean said. "I can see it in the way they look at each other and reach for each other. It's in their actions and their words."

And everyone could see it in Dean's beautiful drawing.

Dean turned the page to reveal a picture of Rosie and Leo and their family—biological and found. It was a whole group, one that Tyler felt himself lucky to be a part of, sitting at a table sharing food, Rosie and Leo at the head. Dean explained how they were the glue of their family that bound it together with love.

He went through several pages, each picture detailed and beautiful.

Tyler tried to gauge Rosie and Leo's response not only to Dean's speech but also to the incredible art. Rosie had her hand over her mouth, her eyes glistening, and Leo was full-on crying again.

Dean turned to the last page. It was a drawing of Rosie and Leo on the gravel road into Silverbrite Springs minutes before the avalanche. In it, Rosie was in the foreground, glowing and excited despite the rain, and Leo was standing on a boulder, pointing toward the glacier. It was like Dean had drawn a snapshot from Tyler's memory of that day.

Tyler remembered dread and discomfort and panic. But that had not been Rosie or Leo's reaction at all.

"This day, where Tyler and I were separated from Rosie and Leo by an avalanche, was one of the scariest of my life," Dean said, his voice wistful. "But Rosie and Leo viewed it as a grand adventure. An obstacle to tackle and overcome and, most importantly, enjoy. In their eyes that day, I saw their future. A lifetime of caring, family, and exploration together. A perfect match. So please raise your glasses."

Everyone lifted their champagne flutes.

Dean met Tyler's eyes through the small crowd. "May we all be so lucky to surround ourselves with love that knows us, sees us, celebrates us, and fights for us. To Rosie and Leo's grand adventure together."

The guests clinked their glasses and said, "Cheers!"

Dean handed the book he'd created to Leo and Rosie and accepted their hugs, but he quickly extricated himself from the crowd and found Tyler.

Tyler grabbed his hand. "I'm so proud of you." It had taken a lot of late-night pep talks to convince Dean that a gift of drawings was the best way to celebrate Rosie and Leo.

"I need something harder than champagne to drink. I feel sick," Dean said.

"Here. Let's go for a quick walk."

Tyler started to lead Dean away from the gathering, but Sarg, who had been assisting the photographer by holding her extra camera, shouted, "Don't go far. You could fall in a hole and die. Pools that look like shallow puddles can be hundreds of feet deep on a glacier."

"Jesus," Tyler muttered, waving a hand at Sarg so he knew they'd heard him. "Remind me again why we keep coming to this death trap of a state."

"Because it's where we fell in love," Dean said. They stepped carefully up a raised edge to see what was beyond. From their higher perspective, Skipper Lake, full of huge icebergs, was visible.

Yeah, Tyler could certainly see the appeal. Spring in Alaska had been nice, but summer was extraordinary.

"You fell in love within four days? What fairytale were you living in, sweetheart? That's too fast," Tyler said.

Dean laughed and squeezed his hand. Dean melted when Tyler called him *sweetheart*. It was another aspect of their relationship that had taken time to come easily to Tyler—like trust and sharing a toothbrush—but he was all in now. No doubts, no overthinking. Tyler's soul was settled. The end.

"I knew I was in trouble before we kissed," Dean said.

"You want to know the moment for me? The point of no return?" Tyler asked.

"Yes, of course."

"It was a few months into dating. You had a chance to answer a bonus question at trivia night about the four valves in the heart. And I thought to myself, *I love* his *heart.*

You got the question wrong, and I didn't even care. The depth of your heart, the incalculability of it, is unmatched. I'll never let you forget that."

"Fuck. Come here." Dean tugged Tyler closer, and Tyler's foot skidded on the ice.

Dean grabbed him and held him to his chest. They were both breathing hard. Tyler didn't have a good record when it came to falling in Alaska, and falling on a glacier was evidently way more dangerous than slipping in the glacial silt it had left behind at Chum Smoke Cabins thousands of years ago.

"You always have to swoop in and save me," Tyler joked once his heart wasn't trying to make an escape through his mouth. "Maybe this *is* a fairytale. You're the knight."

"No." Dean lifted Tyler's chin and kissed him, first on the forehead, then the lips. "We'll save each other, always."

Author's Note

FREE BONUS SCENE

I hope you enjoyed reading *Spring Breakup* as much as I enjoyed writing it. Want to see the moment Tyler realized he was in love with Dean in the middle of a trivia night? Check out a free bonus scene available to my newsletter subscribers!

You can sign up for my newsletter at erinmclellan.com.

WHAT TO READ NEXT

Check out the rest of my kinky **So Over the Holidays series**. All the books are low-angst, fluffy, sex positive, and full of toys! Start with the queer m/f Christmas story, ***Stocking Stuffers***, or the m/m Valentine's Day story, ***Candy Hearts***!

You might also enjoy ***Perfect Matcha***, my m/m best-friends-to-lovers, standalone novella in the Bold Brew shared universe. It has lots of sex toys and role play.

Acknowledgments

The biggest thanks to the readers who have loved and supported the So Over the Holidays series. I am so thankful I'm able to continue writing in this world.

All the cheers to Susie Selva for amazing editing, M.A. Hinkle for impeccable proofreading, Cate Ashwood for a wonderful cover, Karen for coffeeshop dates, and Layla and Allison for the blurb help and cheerleading.

A special shoutout to my Alaskan friends who helped me with naming some of my characters and settings. You're the best group chat ever.

Hugs and kisses to my family.

Also by Erin McLellan

So Over the Holidays Series

Stocking Stuffers

Candy Hearts

Bottle Rocket

Party Favors

Bold Brew Universe

Perfect Matcha

Farm College Series

Controlled Burn

Clean Break

Love Life Series

Life on Pause

Life of Bliss

Storm Chasers Series

Natural Disaster

Standalones

Small City Heart

"What Happens in Tulsa"

About the Author

Erin McLellan writes contemporary romances that are sweet, super sexy, and emotional. She lives in Alaska with her family. She is a lover of chocolate, camping, hiking, antiquing, gardening, Dr Pepper, and reality TV.

www.ingramcontent.com/pod-product-compliance
Lightning Source LLC
LaVergne TN
LVHW041928090826
845145LV00017B/2297

* 9 7 8 1 7 3 5 0 0 4 9 6 9 *